Against All Instinct

Against All Instinct

Joshua Buller

Contents

Prologue

Life is a precious thing that is often taken for granted. In the hustle and bustle of everyday living, most people just don't realize how their every action is, in fact, a fight for survival. But this wasn't always true.

There is a time forgotten, when humans had to struggle just to feed themselves. Small nomadic tribes roamed a dangerous world where one false step would lead to their demise at the hands of creatures better adapted to the radical landscape.

This is a story of one man from such a group.

* * *

He knew himself as Konta. It was a name he had since the day he could start remembering, a name he had chosen for himself. It was impossible to know what name others had given to him; expressing such an abstract concept as a name to his fellow clansmen was a luxury he and his people couldn't afford.

The very idea of a spoken word was unfathomable, as making noise was akin to calling out to every creature within earshot.

So, it was only in the silent comfort of his mind that he was Konta, and that was good enough for him. He gave names to his kinfolk in a similar fashion, not knowing or caring how they referred to themselves.

There was never a reason for him to consider why his clan only communicated with body signals. As he strode through the grasslands amidst his people, following the subtle signs of the chief he had come to know as Murg, the only thing that was on his mind was the coming year.

Winter had begun to thaw, ushering in the prosperous time of Spring – the time when the most docile of prey would begin to emerge from their long hibernation and find food as the vicious beasts that inhabited Winter retreated to colder climates. His people were no different: With the migration of such monsters as the Razorback Mammoth and Snow Gremlins who detested the growing warmth, Spring was a time when they could stock up on food in preparation for the coming Summer, when food was less plentiful and dangers more abundant.

A chilled wind whipped through the grassland, which was even now still tinted with a mild frost. Konta was protected from the cold bite thanks to his fur, pulled from an Obsidian Panther he had killed a couple of years before. It was his most prized possession, a sign of his capability as a strong, young hunter, and like every member of his tribe who bore the pelt of a beast, he protected it as he would protect his child. Without it, his status in the tribe would be scarce higher than the suckling babes who were carried in the folds of their parents' pelts. Without it, he could not be trusted by the others to be taken on hunting raids for the more dangerous but rewarding creatures that would come in the following months.

Many hours of travel passed before Murg held up his hand and stabbed his walking stick into the ground. The tribe had reached a place he deemed suitable to set up camp – a small grove that had enough foliage to conceal them at a distance, but not so much as to hide any potential predators. Night had already begun to push away what warmth was granted by day's influence, but the party did not waste time fearing the encroaching cold as they hastily unfolded their tents from the backs of the young men who had yet to prove their worth in a hunt. The sturdy poles forged from Everlasting Redwood drove into the ground in a single thrust, their light weight but nearly impervious strength creating a strong foundation for the covers that would ward away the chill tonight. The covers, made of the massive leaves of the Weeping Willow and caulked with the waterproof sap of the same tree, would hold tight against anything less than thunderstorms and squalls.

As the men hurried to erect the tepees, the women were busy preparing the camp with a variety of necessary amenities. They still had some musk from the

Desert Squunck they had killed the previous year. When deployed lightly in a wide circle around the camp, the overwhelming odor created a sort of invisible barrier that was all but impassable by any dangerous creature with a strong sense of smell. While one group hurried to form a perimeter, another was setting up the communal fire pit, which would be used to keep the entire tribe warm during the long, cold night in addition to helping cook all their food. One woman had already cut a square of turf away for the firepit and set it aside: this would be replaced when the tribe moved on, to hide evidence that they had been there. A couple of other tribe members had procured some jagged stones to dig the actual pit out and made haste to finish the pit as the light of day quickly faded. Several more still were sticking more Everlasting Redwood poles into the ground around the pit, upon which they would hang a tarp made from the skin of the Sponge Whale: a creature with skin that could absorb almost any non-solid material and detoxify it, which made it perfect for preventing smoke from escaping the campfire area and alerting predators.

Normally during this process of setting up camp, which Konta knew as the Settling, the hunters of the tribe would be busy trying to track prey for tonight's meal. However, the approach of Spring brought with it a different situation. There was no safer time of year than right now, in the first couple days of Spring. Because of this, the tribe used this brief respite between seasons to throw a festival of sorts in honor of the new year and to strengthen their bonds against the coming hardships. It was the one time of the year when Konta's tribe could laugh and smile and forget, for however precious little time, their daily struggle for survival.

* * *

The fire crackled merrily as the tribe gathered around it, each family bringing something else to share with the tribe during this Time of Settling. One of the tribeswomen, whom Konta knew as Klika, had brought a sweet stew made from some preserved Fruit Bats they had harvested the year prior. Her small boy Klikin occasionally tried to sneak a taste before feeding time, only to be reprimanded by his father, the hunter Konta knew as Klik, much to the amusement of the rest of the tribe.

Across the way, Konta spotted Faygo, a fellow hunter whom he had grown up with. Konta watched as Faygo sat amongst the young women of the tribe, showing off a long, sleeve-like bracelet that he had just been given by Chief Murg while they tousled his shoulder-length blonde hair. Konta felt a little resentment at this – the Chief's bracelet was a sign of favor from Murg that only a choice few hunters were given. Most of the hunters that had the bracelet were much older than Konta and Faygo, both of whom had yet to see twenty Winters pass, yet the chief had seen fit to bestow his blessing on only the latter.

All thoughts of the bracelet left his mind as a soft touch alighted on his shoulder. He turned to see the smiling face of his young wife, whom he had only paired with in the past season. Her bushy brown hair grew so thick and untamed that it tumbled recklessly down her shoulders and past her knees, almost skimming the ground, but there was no mistaking the strong yet delicate body that hid beneath. Konta's face broke into an embarrassing smirk, his happiness and pride impossible to hide – he had finally earned what every man of the tribe coveted, a mate. In his mind, she was Kontala, the second half of his personal clan, and Konta could hardly bear waiting for his first pup to be born.

Indeed, they had wasted no time in sealing their partnership, as evidenced by the slight swelling of Kontala's belly. She sat down gingerly beside Konta, resting her head against his shoulder. With a sweep of her hand, she drew the hood of his pelt from his head and ran her fingers through the mess of black locks he normally kept concealed, eliciting a goofy grin from him as the rest of the tribe present laughed silently behind their hands and shook their heads. Normally such displays of affection between mates were awkward amongst other members of the tribe, but they had only partnered less than a season – their newfound affection and lust for each other was considered pardonable. Konta didn't care what they thought anyways. Before long, he would be out of the village often on hunts for food and supplies to see the tribe through the coming seasons, which would be far harsher and more merciless than the calm of Spring. He figured the least the clan could do for him was give such a dedicated warrior one peaceful night with his wife.

The fire had just started to simmer down when Murg finally crept through the folds of the tarp, his face wrinkled and impassive. Konta always marveled at the chief's pelt, a coat covered in feathers with a deep ash coloring. Konta had never seen a creature with such a mantle in all his hunts and knew that, from Murg's position as chief, there was a good reason he hadn't seen it. Likely it came off a rare beast Murg had hunted in seasons long before Konta lived.

The chief's appearance signaled that it was time to eat, and the women bustled to portion out their remaining provisions. The men remained seated, their rough hands forged through years of hunting ill-suited to handle the delicate foods that the women had labored to prepare. Like all their "festivals" past, there was little in way of noisy fanfare and jubilation. They ate in silent gratitude and watched the pups, too young to hunt or work, run around the fire and play. To the hunters, though, tonight was the calm before the storm.

Konta sighed as he thought of the coming days and seasons, where simply waking up each morning would be a miracle to be thankful for. On this night, however, with Kontala's hand in his and with his tribesmen all around him, he felt like there was no obstacle in this world he and his people couldn't overcome.

Tomorrow brings a new day and new challenges.

The Fruit Bat

There was no guaranteed sanctity in sleep for the nomads, who had to constantly keep guard against nocturnal prowlers. Each coming dawn was hardly any safer, as most of the tribe that wasn't keeping watch was still groggy from sleep, and the first glimmers of daylight made them easy to find for those early hour hunters. However, with the advent of Spring, there was a reliable amount of safety with the precautions taken the other day. They relished it while they could; in the coming seasons, such safety would be a rare commodity.

Konta was one of the few men who awoke with the women, who had to rise before the Sun's earliest rays to bring the village up to speed. The hunters were allowed to sleep later as to conserve strength for the trials they would have to face in the coming day; the safety and vitality of the village depended on them being in their top form. However, Konta thrived with only a little sleep, so oftentimes would watch guard until late yet rise earliest, more refreshed and prepared than any other hunter.

Today was especially important to him. It was the day that the young boys of the village would be taken on their first hunt, to prepare them for the trials they'd face to earn their manhood. It was the ideal time to do so, with the dangerous beasts of Winter retreating to colder climates and the deceptive and cunning beasts of Summer yet to fully awaken from their hibernation. In particular, there was one beast that thrived during Autumn that would be ripe for the picking during this time. That was their target today.

The other hunters finally stirred from their slumber, stepping sleepily from their tents as they made their way towards the basins the women had heated for communal bathing. A quick scrub in nearly boiling water woke them up readily enough, and before long they gathered around the meal prepared much earlier that morning, a feast of various scraps from the celebration held the other night.

Konta had already eaten and was, instead, inside his hut preparing the tools they would need for this journey: a flint knife honed to its sharpest and well tested, and a spit made from Everlasting Redwood with the end sharpened to a point and burned black to harden it. The knife would be the only tool they needed for this particular hunt, but the spear would be necessary to ward off any unwanted intrusions. There was another favorite tool of Konta's that sat wrapped, inconspicuous, in a small corner of the hut, but he ignored it for today. It would be too cumbersome to bring along for a hunt where discretion was more important than brute force.

As he prepared to leave the tent, Kontala stepped in with surprising grace. Being with child, her duties were lighter than those of the other women, and she was given frequent rest periods to tend to her own health. As she entered, her eyes alighted on Konta's tools, and a glowing smile crossed her face. Konta, seeing her, could only beam back as he strode forward on powerful legs and swept her into an embrace. Taking his hand in hers, she led him to her belly, where even now their progeny was stirring faintly. Konta marveled at how Kontala could read his emotions so clearly. Today he would be helping the other families' boys learn to become men, but in short time he would finally have a pup of his own to teach the ways of the land – a day that he waited for with bated fervor.

The embrace was quick, but not hurried. Konta let go and made to stride out of the tent, but one hand lingered on his mate's shoulder as he pulled away, only slipping off when he had stepped too far to reach out further. He could feel her eyes following him until he was completely out of sight, and that thought filled him with a vim and vigor greater than any amount of sleep or food could bring; he was ready for today.

The village boys had already gathered around the covered fire pit, each one nervously gripping at the flint knife that their fathers had hewn over the last

11

several days. Some of the hunters were already waiting impatiently near their pups, while those without children were still trickling in. Konta, being one of the latter, stood a good distance from the small huddle of parents and pups as he twirled his knife idly.

It was only a couple minutes after the last of the pups and hunters had entered the tarp when a giant of a man parted a curtain, stepping halfway into the enclosure before throwing himself into a sitting position onto the floor. It was obvious to anyone who saw him why he did this – so massive was the man that even sitting cross-legged on the floor his head came up to the chin of the average hunter. On his back was a pelt of brown spines that appeared to have the texture of felt but clearly had knife-like edges. This man drew the attention of every man and child in that tent, for there wasn't a person in the tribe who didn't recognize the skill of the Head Hunter, whom Konta knew as Zanzu: the man who single-handedly killed the deadly king of Winter, the Razorback Mammoth.

Zanzu's eyes darted over the group, and Konta watched as he took a mental tally of everyone there. It was one of the traits a highly skilled hunter was supposed to have: remembering every member of a large hunting party and making sure all were accounted for at all times. In mere moments, he was finished and stood as he beckoned with a hand for the group to follow his lead. Konta couldn't help but notice the armband he wore, and for the briefest moment felt a pang of jealousy. There was no time for such worthless emotions, though. The hunt was on.

The village scouts had already found their prey the previous night, a task that was only fit for those who had learned to move with the stealth and cunning of the vicious night beasts. Getting there was a simple task, but this was a training hunt, so the pace they made was halved as the more experienced hunters were set to the task of showing the pups how to move without disturbing the forestry or leaving tracks, silently warning what plants were poisonous or, in some cases, carnivorous and thus should be avoided. Fortunately, their destination was not far from where they had set up camp, and even at half-pace it took less than the span of the afternoon to arrive.

Before the pack was a grove of trees that stretched a fair deal higher than their neighbors. Konta recognized these as Skyscraper Cedars, trees that grew indefinitely until they could no longer bear their own weight and were sent toppling to the ground. Of course, he also was aware of the creature that made Skyscrapers their nests during the Spring season, due to their risky propagation methods.

Even now, the hunters were addressing the pups mutely, gesturing to a small number of objects that appeared attached to the trunks of the half-dozen trees in this grove. They were brightly colored orbs, about the size of a young man's head. Zanzu reached up towards one that no other hunter could reach while standing and held it with the care one would hold a newborn with. His other hand grasped his knife and blurred through the air as he slashed between the tree and the strange orb, separating the object from the trunk almost effortlessly. He lowered it for the young ones to observe, and now they saw that the orb was actually placental in nature, clear and filled with a colorful liquid. In the center was a small, featureless embryo – the fetus of a Fruit Bat.

Konta had hunted Fruit Bats before. Flying beasts that in adulthood boasted wingspans equivalent to five adults standing and were able to produce their own food supplies internally provided they had enough water. Konta had named them from the sweet taste their flesh produced – a taste shared by the pods of their young. These primarily nocturnal monsters prospered during the endless rain of Autumn, where they could hunt without rest for days. Fortunately, they migrated to unknown lands to hibernate during Summer and Winter, returning during Spring only long enough to spawn their brood that would gestate over several months, finally emerging in Autumn to start their own lives.

Sure enough, Konta's keen eyes scanned the canopy of the Skyscrapers until they finally landed on a large figure concealed within the shadows of the leaves. The adult Fruit Bat was currently sleeping, worn out from having planted its young on the tree. The Fruit Bat pods, connected securely to the trunk, would draw nutrients from the tree to complete their growth. However, these placentas were filled with a nutrient-rich material in which the embryo developed, a perfect food source for any creature careful enough to not invoke the wrath of a sleep deprived mother Fruit Bat.

Each other hunter took turns demonstrating how to harvest the Fruit Bat young: slowly climbing up the tree, supporting the pod while separating the thin mucous veins that drew forth nutrients, and carefully handling the pod lest the delicate membrane around it puncture.

The hunters had made their demonstration while climbing to the higher placentas, leaving the lower ones alone to make it easier for the less developed pups to be able to reach. The adults each took a small number of the fledgling hunters and watched them take turns climbing up and separating. As was normal, the children took quickly to the teachings, but failure was not treated kindly. Every pod that was broken or dropped was rebuked with a firm but quiet blow from the child's father; it was necessary for the pups to learn that wasting the life of a creature and gaining nothing was not tolerable.

Finally, each child stood with a placenta in hand, making sure they held it as carefully as possible. The full-fledged hunters made show of their skills by deftly harvesting the remaining Fruit Bat pods, leaving one per tree, in the highest reaches of the canopy where they'd be concealed and safe from other predators. Konta learned through years of experience that by doing this, the Fruit Bat embryos would not be competing with each other for the tree's precious nutrients and would grow much more quickly. This would lead to a choice few strong, hardy Fruit Bats, rather than numerous weaker ones. The strong ones would definitely thrive, making sure that they'd have more pods to harvest for many Springs to come.

They left the mature Fruit Bat sleeping, not wanting to rouse it with so many young, inexperienced targets that were just as ripe for the picking as the pods. The harvest they had today would make fine meals for days to come, with yet more of them set to be preserved for use when food supplies ran low. It was a successful venture today, something that Konta knew was rare for a hunt. He glanced around at the content faces of the children, who seemed genuinely proud of their achievements, and knew that not all of them would live through the coming seasons, as their instincts would be tested time and again against far more dangerous fare. For now, though, they would have this small victory. That, Konta knew, they deserved at least.

The Fauxbe Cow

Normally, the tribe did not stay active during night-time. The risks were simply too high for the rewards, since it was during such time that dangerous creatures that reveled in the darkness came out to hunt. However, there was a small enclave of hunters in the tribe who could move freely during the night, using their superior cunning and mobility to find prey for the next day's hunt. These were the scouts, and they were the pride of the tribe, for without their prowess in night hunting, the day hunters would have no information on where a den of predators might be or where potential prey lay waiting, ripe for the plucking.

Such was the situation that Konta found himself in as he was silently woken while the Moon still hung high over the canopy. As a safe practice, it was two sharp taps on his shoulder that woke him. Sleepy as he was, Konta recognized this as a sign that he was being stirred out of sleep by a tribesman, rather than some creature sampling him as prey.

The one who was standing over him was his friend Klik, one of the more seasoned tribal scouts. The hood of Klik's pelt was pulled low over his head, and if Konta hadn't seen it so many times he might have startled at the sight of the massive compound eyes that now glared at him – the eyes of the Wonderwasp. Klik knew how unsettling this sight was, though, and quickly lowered his hood, allowing Konta to see the excitement in his eyes. Konta had seen this expression before and knew what being woken so early meant: the scouts had found an opportunity so great that it couldn't wait until morning.

Konta hadn't had much sleep, having been on late guard duty again. The Moon had only moved three finger spans since Konta had laid down for the night. Still, he had known Klik for a long time, and Konta was quite aware that, if his friend woke him, then there was good reason for it.

He rose with care, making sure not to rouse Kontala from her much needed rest, and quickly dressed himself. As he draped his Obsidian Panther pelt over his shoulders, Klik approached him and handed him a weapon. Konta took pause as he took the tool in hand. It was a fairly normal looking hammer with a shaft as long as Konta's forearm and a hammerhead slightly larger than his fist. However, it was the head of this tool that was unlike anything else in the tribe – it shone with a luster like the surface of the water in the midday Sun, a color more beautiful than any stone seen before.

Konta had found this sparkling stone several years prior and learned soon thereafter that it bore strength enough to smash solid rock without breaking. It took many seasons for him to work a hole in it and fit a handle inside, but upon doing this, Konta came into possession of a weapon of unparalleled efficiency. It was this weapon alone that had secured many of Konta's recent kills and cemented his place as a top hunter. It would be unfair to consider this turn of events unfair luck on Konta's part: the rules of the tribe might have been unspoken, but they were followed absolutely. His fortune was considered part of his hunting skill, just as much as the muscles he earned through years of hard effort.

Despite its unquestionable strength, Konta was often reluctant to bring the weapon with him on hunts. Simply put, it was too heavy – on long hunts, it sapped Konta's strength to carry it with him, and swinging it repeatedly would tire even his strong body quickly. It was a tool to be used only when a single, devastating blow would guarantee a kill. The hammer was all but worthless against prey that was nimble or expected to require a prolonged chase. The fact that Klik handed this weapon to Konta meant that this was the situation that was presented now. Konta's hammer was the most effective tool for this hunt, and so Konta- sleep deprived as he was – would be needed for this particular hunt.

Konta was tying the hammer to his waist as he stepped out of his tepee and approached the covered fire pit where a small number of shadowed silhouettes had already gathered. The fire had been put out quite some time ago, but Konta's eyes had long since adjusted to the darkness, and he could make out three other hunters. Besides Klik, there was Bobo, another scout like Klik who wore the pelt of an adult Fruit Bat. Standing next to Bobo was a young man who Konta recognized as Bobo's son, Bobobu. Normally a small group such as this would be used to hunt during a night hunt, as a large group would make too much noise and draw unwanted attention, but Konta was confused by Bobobu's presence. A hunter without a pelt wouldn't usually be brought along on such a risky hunt, but Konta got the feeling that Bobo was bringing his son along precisely so he could finally get his first pelt – Bobobu was of the age where he was expected to bag a hunt on his own, after all. Konta had the feeling the only reason he was coming along was to lend his hammer.

Klik and Bobo took the lead as the group set out to the site they found. Bobo quickly found a tall tree and scampered up it without making a sound. Once he reached the top, he unfurled from within the folds of his cloak a pair of giant, membranous wings. The frames that had been built into them by the tribeswomen snapped into place, creating a makeshift glider, and with the grace of a thousand flights' experience, Bobo took to the sky, the natural design of the Fruit Bat's wings allowing him to soar silently through the night sky. No matter how many times Konta saw it, he couldn't deny it was a spectacle to see and a credit to the ingenuity of the women of the tribe. He smiled as he saw the dumbfounded look on Bobobu's face; clearly, he had never seen his father's expertise in action before.

Meanwhile, Klik led the other two on the ground. The wings of the Wonderwasp couldn't grant him flight like Bobo, but Konta knew that the large, bulbous eyes on the hood of Klik's pelt granted him absolute vision in all directions. Klik would see any threat, no matter what angle it came at from the ground, and Bobo's aerial scouting would allow him to see danger that lay outside Klik's panoramic view. There was almost no enemy their combined talents couldn't detect, and more than once it was these skills that had saved the tribe from utter destruction.

The Moon had traveled several more finger spans before Klik held up a hand to stop Konta and Bobobu. Bobo had been circling around an area a fair distance ahead, and Konta knew what this meant: that was where their prey waited. After a few more circles, Bobo returned, alighting in a tree with unnatural agility before disconnecting the struts holding his wings firm and returning them to the depths of his cowl. He scampered down the tree easily and joined with his comrades. Bobobu began to breathe heavily, perhaps nervously. Bobo quickly saw this and laid a reassuring hand on his son's shoulders. Konta could only imagine how the two must have felt, at this critical junction in Bobobu's life, and for a moment his thoughts returned to his mate, asleep in their tent. There was little time for selfish thoughts, though, for Konta still did not know what they were about to encounter.

That question was answered readily enough as Klik led them to the edge of the forest, where they now overlooked a small grassy meadow. In the middle of it was a creature that filled Konta with a rush of excitement.

The Kogyu Cow was a beast of fortune to the tribe, one rarely found and even more rarely hunted successfully. They were even more reclusive than Konta's tribe, dwelling in small herds far from the eyes of watchful predators, and for good reason: their meat was by far one of the most delectable and nutritious of any beast that existed. Konta had no idea why this was. The lifestyle of the Kogyu was shrouded in mystery, but whatever their routine was certainly also would explain the secret to their desirability.

The one thing that Konta did know of them was that this routine was extremely strict, from eating to mating to sleeping. The only time Kogyu were known to break their routines were when their herds were found, in which case they would quickly relocate to avoid utter extermination. Konta's tribe discovered long ago that their behavior was so deeply ingrained, the Kogyu would fall asleep at the same time every night, regardless of location. This was the only way that one could be caught under most circumstances- when one strayed from the herd, whether from immaturity or injury, and ended up falling asleep elsewhere.

This seemed to be the case now, as the group laid eyes on a young bovine slumbering in the middle of the meadow, its nose pressed firmly to the ground. No doubt it had gotten separated and ended up grazing until it ultimately went comatose, just as its heritage dictated. This was a catch beyond their wildest expectations: so nutritious was the Kogyu Cow's meat that a small bite could feed a normal man for a whole day, to say nothing of how many seasons a tribe could feast off an entire Kogyu.

Bobo wordlessly sidled alongside Konta and held a hand out. Konta understood immediately and handed his hammer to the scout, its head glinting in the moonlight. Bobo, in turn, handed the weapon to his son, who staggered ever so slightly from the surprising weight it possessed. Over the next couple of minutes, Bobo gestured towards the slumbering Kogyu, using subtle gestures to 'tell' Bobobu the proper way to approach the quarry. All the while, Konta and Klik kept vigilant for predators, but luck seemed to be on their side this night. Not the slightest sound or disturbance indicated danger about.

Finally, Bobobu took a deep, calming breath and started towards his quarry. Konta was already well versed in how to hunt a Kogyu, despite only having hunted the beast on one other occasion: They possessed upwards of three times the strength of the average hunter, so approaching them from the front or back would only result in being horribly trampled or kicked, respectively. The best way to approach was from the side, as they turned slowly, and therefore, it'd be easier to react to any aggression they showed. Sure enough, Bobobu took slow, measured steps as he swung around towards the side, raising the hammer over his head so he would be ready to deliver a single decisive blow the moment he came within striking range.

Konta hadn't realized just how lightheaded he was from being woken so abruptly, but there were details tugging at the edge of his subconscious that started to bother him. Normally, Kogyu were all but impossible to find during Spring, as their mating season was during Autumn and that was usually when there was the highest chance of one being separated from its herd. Even more concerning was how marshy the ground was under their feet. The ground was still spongy with the moisture of Winter's melting snow, and that was something that disconcerted Konta for some reason.

It finally dawned on him what he had forgotten about, but the moment he realized the danger of the situation, there came a horrific cry in the night. It was the sound most terrifying to the people of the tribe: the sound of one of their own in pain.

Right as Bobobu came within killing distance of the Kogyu, the beast swung sideways at a completely impossible angle, appearing to balance perfectly on its nose while all four of its legs wrapped around the young hunter. They tightened instantly into a vice-like grip, the sound of snapping bones popping through the otherwise silent night as Bobo's son let out an involuntary shriek of agony. Now the Kogyu lifted its nose from the ground, revealing a long appendage attached where the mouth should have been. A gruesome, fanged maw emerged nearby, its teeth gnashing eagerly at the fresh meat now flailing nearby.

Without hesitation, Konta lunged forward. Bobobu had dropped his hammer in the shock of the attack, but unlike the fledgling hunter, Konta had practiced many hours with the weapon. In a single swift motion, he hoisted the weighted head over his own and brought it down on the toothy visage. The beast's face caved in at the impact, teeth scattering in all directions as their former owner howled detestably and retreated to the ground. The false Kogyu promptly released its victim, sliding into the marshy soil with unnerving ease.

Konta shook with fear and rage: how could he forget about the terrifying trap of the Fauxbe Cow? Though almost as rare to encounter as the genuine article itself, any appearance of a Kogyu had to be inspected, lest this predator of opportunity lay in waiting.

In spite of the name Konta had given it, the creature was far closer to a mole than a cow. It lived deep within the ground, using its large hand to burrow through soft soil until it was ready to attempt feeding. The monster was a gluttonous carnivore but had an exceedingly weak body save for its single, absurdly powerful tunneling hand. In order to trap prey, this powerful hand had evolved extraordinarily to appear as something that all beasts desired: the Kogyu Cow. Once an unsuspecting predator came within range, the Fauxbe would grab hold of the victim and paralyze them with the weak venom their saliva contained. At that point, it was only a matter of time.

The surge of adrenaline had snapped Konta wide awake, and now he was well aware of the horrible danger their group was in. The Fauxbe Cow had already bitten Bobobu by the time Konta smashed in the beast's face. The boy's leg was bleeding profusely, another property of the Fauxbe's venom, and his cry had carried for miles. There was one thing every member of the tribe knew well – all creatures of the world favored human flesh above all other foods, and Bobobu had basically announced a feast for anything within earshot.

Konta bolted from the spot as fast as he could with his heavy weapon still in tow. It was the only tool he had brought with him, and to go unarmed into the wilderness would be worse than standing around at this point. Klik understood the situation just as well, and took a stride ahead of Konta, frantically looking around for any beast that was trying to cut them off. They couldn't stop to see if Bobo was following suit. If he stayed to help his offspring, then his life was forfeit – Konta and Klik favored preserving their own lives above all else now.

They barely broke pace as they passed over the odorous barrier of Desert Squunck musk set up several weeks prior. Once within the boundary of the tepees, they quickly got the attention of the guards and alerted them to the danger that there might soon be an attack from some predator, whatever it may be.

Several hours later, after the Moon had already passed beyond the horizon, the entire tribe stood awake in the covered fire pit, the children wide-eyed and frightened and all adults, man and woman alike, armed and waiting for any threat that may approach.

It was only after the Sun began to peek out that there was any stir of life other than the fearful tribesmen. A large shadow swooped overhead, but the hunters refrained from spearing it as Bobo landed a distance off from the fire pit, his face gaunt and pale. He was alone.

The people knew that no scout who was chosen for the position would ever return to the camp if there was a chance of being tailed, but they were still left with no choice. They would have to spend the coming day packing, always watching out for attacks, before moving on. It was much sooner than they would normally, but their safety was compromised.

Konta cursed himself inwardly for his ignorance and hindsight. He should have seen the dangers of the Fauxbe, even if the monster was so rare to encounter. He should have recognized that the ground was soft enough for it to tunnel through, lying in wait for anything looking for easy prey to wander by, or the way the "nose" of the Kogyu was buried just a little bit deeper than normal. These are things that a scout couldn't easily spot, as Fauxbe Cows were not normally nocturnal hunters, but a day hunter such as Konta was well aware that anomalies such as last night were something to always be wary for, and now they paid the price. They lost a promising young hunter, and it would be many seasons before this wound would scar over – for Konta or for Bobo.

The Canteen Turtle

There had been precedent for the tribe leaving a campsite earlier than planned, but it didn't make it any less frustrating and added an unnecessary hardship to the tribe's strenuous life. Rest areas that were relatively safe and near sources of food were scarce as it was, so being forced to leave one prematurely was a heavy blow to morale.

The tribe was no stranger to travel. It was their very nature to pick up and move on with the changing of the seasons, finding more temperate climates to live through the harsh weather changes that came naturally with each season. Even so, the dangers the tribe faced were increased when on the move. Every step they took was another chance they would leave a telltale sign to a wary predator that they had been there; and when the tribe could only move as quickly as its slowest member, it always made travel a risky venture.

What was more troubling was how rapidly the seasonal shift seemed to be occurring, and Konta could tell that something was off right away. As Spring gave way to Summer, the plants that thrived in the former would quickly wilt from the rapid climate changes, and the harsh, dry winds of the latter brought with them fierce sandstorms that would eventually blanket the ground where rich foliage had only days before stood. Normally, this transition was slow and gradual, and the first appearance of dying plants would be the signal to pick up and move. As the tribe moved ever onward, however, Konta started noticing some disconcerting signs.

The flora that had been lush and green near their old camp just a couple days before had already turned a decrepit shade of brown, leaves peeling off constantly and falling to the ground where they cracked and dissolved, dry and brittle. The tribe was also moving even slower than usual since a thin layer of dust had begun to accumulate on the forest floor. Every step left footprints that the rear guard had to make sure and cover. There was no doubt in Konta's mind that Summer would be here sooner than anticipated, and even with their early departure, there would be little chance of them reaching the valley where they usually weathered out Summer in time. They would have to prepare for a worst-case scenario.

Sidling up besides Faygo and nudging him, Konta made a gesture to the plants that were visibly deteriorating, some of them already ripping free of their desiccated, useless roots and threatening to fall. Faygo nodded, and Konta knew he must have come to the same conclusion: Summer would be upon them within days, and they would be blindsided if they were not ready.

Thus, the two approached the chief, who was already eyeballing the same things that Konta was observing. Murg looked upon them for a few moments, holding up a hand to stop the convoy of villagers as Konta watched the old man's mind work furiously, trying to figure out what the best course of action would be at this time. Finally, Murg tapped the chest of three hunters, a sign that he had a hunt for them: Konta, Klik, and surprisingly, Bobo.

Bobo had been a wreck since his return from the Fauxbe Cow's trap. Konta found it hard to sympathize with him, as death was a necessary risk every hunter faced in order to help the tribe. Obviously, losing a hunter was a detriment to the group, but each death only instilled in the other hunters a greater sense of importance in preparation and caution during hunts. Of course, Konta also realized that the loss of a son might be something more profound than he could understand right now, especially one with so much promise. When he looked to his dear Kontala, her belly growing more with each passing day, he thought of what his feelings would be should some predator attack her and their unborn child. Just a passing thought about it made his blood boil, and he suddenly found it hard to think any further ill of Bobo's current state of mind.

Perhaps this was why Murg chose Bobo for the mission. The once unflinching hunter needed to be reminded of what his role was in the tribe and what the pelt he wore signified. The tribe needed him now, more than ever.

The chief was quick to give his order. He picked up a handful of sand from the ground and tossed it, creating a billowing cloud of dust. Then he nodded at Bobo. The message might have seemed abstract, but it was a simple and silent way to get the message across: Bobo was to find a large amount of sand right away. He was to look for a desert.

Bobo, ragged as he looked, wasted no time in climbing the tallest tree he could find and extending the Fruit Bat wings, taking to the sky as he had so many hundreds of times before. As he disappeared over the withering canopy, Murg crouched to the ground and hastily sketched a crude picture in the sand with his finger, one large oval with three smaller ovals to represent a head and feet. Then he grabbed a small hide flask from his side and dripped a tiny amount of water onto the picture.

Konta's spine chilled as he realized what the chief was asking for, but he also realized that there was no other option. For their clan to survive the merciless Summer, they would need a constant supply of water, and there was only one way to get a sure supply of it for the season to come.

What they needed was a Canteen Turtle.

Konta noticed that one of Klik's eyes narrowed ever so slightly. He, too, understood what they were going after and also understood the danger they were about to be put up against. For them to get what they needed from the creature, they'd have to bring it back alive, and the tribe would need at least a couple to sustain everyone. To find a Canteen Turtle was one thing, but capturing one was a task that was as dangerous as accosting a Razorback Mammoth. Konta was curious as to why the chief didn't decide to send a more distinguished hunter in his stead. Bobo and Klik both bore the bracelets that Murg bestowed on those hunters he favored, but Konta had not yet accomplished whatever enigmatic task the chief sought in a warrior to bless him with one.

Another thought quickly crossed his mind. Perhaps this was what would finally prove himself worthy of that bracelet, and Konta could finally become a hunter the entire tribe could be proud of. This was the hope he nurtured as Bobo returned, landing perhaps a little heavier than normal, but not enough to endanger their position. A quick gesture with his hand indicated the direction of their destination, and considering how quickly he had returned, it wasn't far off. Perhaps luck was finally beginning to trickle back to the tribe.

The other tribesmen hurried to procure wrappings for the hunters, thick robes and face scarves that would protect them from the Sun's vicious heat. Once secured in their protective clothing, they wrapped their pelts back over their bodies and set out with Bobo in the lead, Konta only stalling for the briefest moment to glance back at his mate, who nodded encouragingly. It was the small gestures like those that gave Konta the fiery determination to come back alive, no matter the cost.

The Sun had just crested past midday when the trio emerged from the quickly ruining forest onto an open sand dune. It was a stark reminder of how harrowing the change between seasons was; the desert started just as abruptly as the forest ended, and Konta almost felt that, if he looked closely enough, he could see as the desert slowly encroached on the wilderness and swallowed it up. There was little time to waste pondering the fury of Nature now, though. They still had a turtle to find in all this sand.

The Canteen Turtle was known to live in sheltered oases in the desert, where they would be unimpeded in their growth. While it may sound like this was the perfect opportunity for any parched scavenger, their existence was undercut by something far more sinister. The Turtles were as safe as could be, and their protection was what sent another chill of primal fear through Konta and his companions.

Without the trees to take the brunt of the desert winds, the hunters had to rely on their thick wrappings and pelts to protect them from the constant buffeting of the desert zephyrs. While they were shielded from most of the heat beating down on them, it wasn't long before the effects of prolonged heat exposure began to creep up on them. They drank small amounts regularly, giving Konta a slight bit more, for the jet-black fur of his Obsidian Panther pelt absorbed heat readily and thus caused him to overheat rapidly. There was no place for him to stow it, though, and the other alternative – leaving it behind – was out of the question while he was hunting, so he suffered in silence and did his best to conserve strength as they approached a likely area from which to spot their prey.

Once again, luck was on their side as they reached the top of a particularly large dune. The type of oasis that Canteen Turtles frequented tended to be located in deep valleys created by a number of large sand dunes. Sure enough, at the bottom of the hill they now stood on, another slightly smaller dune rose in the middle. At the top of that one rested a gentle pool of water, surrounded by three palm trees and some rough brush. It was likely a Canteen Turtle nest.

The next step was where they would have to move cautiously. Once they started their procurement of the Turtles, there was no going back, and one false move would spell certain death for all party members involved. The three looked at each other, each thinking up their own plan.

Konta knew that he was likely the fastest runner in the shifting sands of the desert, but Bobo would probably be faster flying. Bobo couldn't fly with the added weight of the Canteen Turtle slowing him down, though, so if that was to be an option, it would be down on Klik and Konta to get the Turtles.

Bobo appeared to notice Konta looking at the Fruit Bat pelt and shook his head as he touched the soft brown fur. Konta got the message – Bobo had no intention of flying. Konta figured that Bobo maybe would have trouble moving properly in the fierce winds, and there was a very real danger of crashing if he couldn't control his glider. Instant death.

It was then that Klik tapped his own pelt and raised an eyebrow, indicating he would serve as the bait needed for the all-important distraction.

There was a trait to the Wonderwasp that wasn't readily apparent during the night when Klik was usually out scouting. The large winged insect was actually a Summer beast, successfully hunting in the harsh deserts thanks to its brilliant carapace. When the plates of the Wonderwasp were struck by sunlight, they bounced back in every color of a prism, shimmering and twisting in a way that confused potential predators and, at the same time, induced a mild form of hypnosis in prey with weaker constitutions.

Konta, even now, had to be careful not to stare directly at the pelt, lest its luster get the best of him. Konta realized that Klik was right and that, if they had any hope of escaping with their prey, Klik would have to be the diversion while Bobo and Konta took the targets.

With their plan formulated, each hunter took a deep, steady breath before descending the dune. They had to be careful not to reveal their presence quite yet. One false alarm would be enough to drive the Turtles completely out of their reach and put the entire tribe in grave danger.

Fortunately, the dunes surrounding the raised oasis created a funnel for the winds, causing them to howl loudly as they passed through. This gave the trio some much desired cover as they reached the dune upon which the oasis stood. Stopping at the base, they looked at each other one last time, nodding solemnly before rushing up the side, scurrying as quickly as they could.

They were halfway up when Konta felt the first tremor. He couldn't stop climbing, though his heart felt like it froze solid in his chest. The rumble quickly subsided, but he knew it would be a short reprieve at best. They had to act now, before their presence was fully revealed.

It took mere moments afterwards to approach the oasis. There was an intense natural beauty to the place. The bushes were greener and more lively than some plants that lived during the Spring; the palm trees that dotted the oasis stood over four men high, large orange fruits lazily hanging from the fronds. The water of the oasis sparkled a dazzling blue, the purest, cleanest water imaginable. In the middle of this crystal-clear water were about ten large, stone-like shapes. They were the reason for this impossibly pure water, the targets of this hunt: the Canteen Turtles.

A second tremor knocked them from their stupor. They had to act fast, because that was the last warning they would get. Konta and Bobo moved forward as gingerly as possible, as if they dared not so much as stir the sand beneath their feet. There was no apparent way to reach the Turtles without stepping in the water, and they had no time to try and think of a different plan, so they did the only thing available and plunged into the waist high lake. The water was cold and felt incredible on their sun-dried bodies, but there was no time to enjoy this blissful sensation. A small, mottled head rose out of the water and let out a shrill shriek as the Canteen Turtle sensed something invading its territory. Within moments, the others had all raised their heads and let out their cry for help as well.

At once, the dune began to shudder, sand now pouring down its slopes, revealing a hard, craggy under-surface. This landmass slowly, very slowly, rose from between the sand dunes, supported by four stumpy legs, each one as wide as six men head to foot. From one of the far ends, a massive, bulky shape emerged from within the giant shell, opening two great, black, beady eyes that blinked against the intense rays of the Sun. Then it opened a mouth that could fit a dozen humans inside easily and let out a bellow that shook the earth.

The Canteen Turtle lived its life with safety from almost all predators because it spent the entirety of its immature years living on the back of its parent. It was a monster that was larger and stronger, pound for pound, than the horrifying Razorback Mammoth – the Tortoasise.

And Konta, Klik, and Bobo had just incurred this mother's wrath.

The Tortoasise

The anger of a disturbed Tortoasise was something that was instilled into hunters of the tribe at the earliest age possible. They were a dangerous existence that was only rivaled by the relentless beasts of Winter, but unlike those, the Tortoasise was a creature that did not actively seek out its prey. A tribe could go the span of a dozen seasons without ever accosting this behemoth of a predator. Still, this was exactly why aspiring hunters had to be taught quickly how to spot the warning signs of a nesting Tortoasise and how to safely navigate past them, for provoking the ire of an adult was at best a death sentence for the hapless fool; at worst, the entire tribe would be left at the mercy – or lack thereof – of its fury.

Konta remembered the day he and a group of other young hunters-to-be were led by a much more seasoned hunter, a man he had named Sinje, to a young Tortoasise during one calmer Summer. It was as perfect a time as they would ever get to be instructed on how to spot one and how to avoid calling its attention to a hunting party. During that incident, only three of the eight fledglings made it back alive, and only because the enraged beast was too distracted killing Sinje and the other five less fortunate young ones. Konta, of course, was among the survivors, and to this day he held a deep fear and respect for the creature and the power it possessed.

This Tortoasise that they now had the misfortune of dealing with was much older than the one he had last seen and, subsequently, was at least twice the size. Its roar shook Konta, Bobo, and Klik to their bones, and there were faint stirs of life in the surrounding area as various other beasts took to flight, lest they be caught in the wake of the monster's rampage. Under regular circumstances, the three hunters would be doing the same. It was only because they weren't dealing with regular circumstances that they were anywhere near this beast in the first place. They needed its brood, no matter the risk.

The task at hand only grew more and more impossible to pull off with each passing moment, as the Tortoasise rose to its full height. From the top of its back to the desert floor was a height of at least one hundred heads. Even if they tried to slide off its back, the bottom of its shell was no less than forty heads from the ground: it would be a sheer drop down. Factoring in that they'd be holding heavy loads that needed to survive the impact as well, and that they'd also be put right in the path of stomping legs the size of tree trunks, the chance of getting away with even one

Canteen Turtle, let alone two of them, was nigh on impossible.

Their plan to use Klik as a distraction was forgotten. In his panic, Konta's mind raced desperately to try and figure out a way down. One of the nearby Canteen Turtles snapped angrily at him, shaking him from his thoughts. As he narrowly avoided losing a leg to its razor-sharp beak, he noticed that this particular one was a deal larger than its brethren. What's more, there were two small leafy buds sprouting from its shell, a trait that it did not share with the other Canteen Turtles.

At once Konta realized that this was the only chance that they had.

Immediately he scanned the area, despite the heaving of the mother underfoot, and found two large, craggy fruits that had fallen off the trees that grew from the Tortoasise's back. These unique fruits were long ago discovered by the tribe to be highly toxic to humans. As droppings from a Tortoasise have never been found, an oddity considering its size, Konta figured that perhaps they were an alternate method of discarding waste from the gargantuan body. What was poisonous to people, however, was the sole food source for the growing Canteen Turtles. Another thing that Konta knew from experience was that Canteen Turtles were ravenous gluttons and wouldn't stop eating when they encountered any foodstuff.

Hastily, Konta found two nearby Turtles and shoved the fruits into their mouths. As expected, they clamped down and began eating immediately. He let out an incoherent shout, normally something a human would never do, but considering the circumstances, there was no chance they could be in any more danger, and it was the only way he could get his comrades' attention. As they looked to him, he picked up one of the Turtles engrossed in eating and shoved it into Bobo's arms. He did the same to Klik with the other Turtle and gave them a stern look that told them he had a plan. The two looked to each other, then back to Konta. Giving brief nods, they knew to trust his judgment; they were well aware of his experience with the Tortoasise, something neither of them had gone through, and decided it was their best bet on getting what they needed.

Once Konta knew their cooperation was assured, he turned back to the turtle with the leaf buds that had tried to bite him earlier and struck it with the flat of his hand. It let out a low cry, far lower than the call its brothers and sisters made. Beneath them, the mother Tortoasise let out another earthshaking bellow. Then, she began to rise up on her hind legs.

This was the break the hunters needed. As it reared back to try and eject the intruders from its back, the hindquarters of the beast lowered almost completely to the ground. Bobo and Klik knew right away that this was the safest descent they'd be given and wasted no time in rushing towards the back end of the gargantuan beast as the platform they stood on quickly became steeper and steeper. Their stride became an involuntary run as the creature rose to a height of over two hundred heads standing, but with a final leap, they hit the ground rolling, the sand thankfully absorbing most of their landing as they did everything they could to protect their precious cargo, which continued to munch away merrily.

Before the Tortoasise had begun to rise, Konta had already slipped on the makeshift sleeves of his Obsidian Panther pelt, which were made from the creature's forelimbs. Still attached to each paw were three long, razor-sharp claws, each as long as Konta's longest finger. As he slipped on the arms of his pelt, he started off towards the creature's head at a sprint, but even at his breakneck pace, he only reached its neck right before it had stood to its full hind-legged height. Furiously, Konta lunged at the scaly neck, sinking both sets of claws into its flesh to find purchase as the creature bucked to and fro to try and dislodge him. His body flailed around helplessly as the Tortoasise fought to throw him from its back, but Konta dug deep and kept his hold for as long as he could. Just as it felt he would be sent sailing to his death, the beast began to heave forward, unable to hold itself upright any longer.

The creature landed back on all fours with such weight that the ground trembled for miles around it. Konta had kicked off backwards the moment it began to descend, lest the force of its landing sent him flying forwards. He landed with a massive splash in the pool where the Tortoasise's brood lived, the creature's movements sloshing its contents everywhere. Still, he couldn't try to escape yet; he had to buy more time for his fellow hunters to make away with their prey.

Konta had seen a lot of incredibly large creatures in his years of hunting and often wondered how such creatures, which had very few predators to threaten them, weren't found all over the place. Certainly, they should have been able to thrive, undeterred, and populate the entire land. It was only after learning about how other creatures mated that he had come to the conclusion that perhaps these giant creatures had troubles reproducing, either because of a rarity of mates or simply that their progeny did not live long enough to reach maturity.

Surely this was the case with the monstrous Tortoasise – the number of individuals ever found in a single season by the tribe could be counted on one hand. Such a giant probably lived for hundreds of years, maybe even thousands, but perhaps this was because their offspring so rarely reached adulthood. Perhaps they needed to live that long so they could produce enough spawn to ensure that one would live long enough to one day propagate themselves.

Yes, Konta had based his entire plan on a mere hunch of the Tortoasise's mating habit. However, this hunch was based on a lifetime of experience gained through life-or-death situations, where understanding the target was the difference between being a predator and being prey. It was those instincts that had allowed him to come this far in his life, and he would trust those instincts once more to get him out of this impossible situation. He had to hope that the

Tortoasise would sacrifice two of its children to protect the one that had begun to fully mature, perhaps
the only one that had grown this far out of hundreds
of broods.

The creature's massive, lumbering body turned
slowly as its head swiveled just in time to see Klik
and Bobo, halfway up a dune, each clutching one of
its children. Konta, sore from the fall, forced himself
to run through the empty lake towards the maturing
Canteen Turtle. Both it and its remaining siblings had
held on during their mother's bucking by clamping
its powerful jaws into the strong tree roots that had
been entangled beneath the water's surface. Swiftly,
Konta pulled his hand back and landed another firm
blow on the head. The creature cried out once more,
which caused the mother to roar and begin to rise
on its hind legs again. Konta's hunch had been cor-
rect: the Tortoasise chose to protect that single ray
of hope to continue its lineage rather than chase two
possible dead ends.

Now all Konta had to do was escape with his life.

The Canteen Turtles had already clamped down
again as the mother began to stand, which gave
Konta some much needed time to prepare for his
flight. From the inside of his pelt, he removed the two
hind legs of the Obsidian Panther, which had been re-
fashioned into leggings. Konta pulled these on, sticking his feet in the slipper-like paws, and after making sure everything was snugly attached, he bent low
and took off for the rear end of the Tortoasise's shell.

The descent was steep, and Konta struggled to keep himself from falling off the massive creature's back and head first into the sand, but thankfully, by the time he could no longer find purchase on the shell, the back end had almost reached the ground anyways, and so with a deft tumble, Konta hit the sand and rolled to his feet.

Without skipping a beat, Konta bolted, not even sparing a glance back. The Tortoasise would notice her attackers had fled momentarily, and the more distance he put between himself and it before it noticed, the better. He stumbled as the creature fell to all fours again, tremors emanating from its landing, but the pads of the Obsidian Panther's paws compacted the sand beneath his feet, keeping him from losing his footing as he righted himself and kept running.

His lungs ached, his muscles were sore, and his bones creaked from having been tossed around so much, but he forced himself to continue onward. Thoughts of his tribesmen, his Kontala, and their unborn child forced him to ignore anything that might slow him down as he dragged himself over the dune back towards where they came from. He thought that the sounds of the giant's footsteps and the shaking under his feet were growing steadily weaker, but he refused to turn around until he had reached the top of the dune and started towards the bottom, at which point his stamina finally caved in and he tumbled to the ground, rolling sideways all the way to the bottom where he lay, covered in sand and completely exhausted. He had made it.

He could no longer hear any stirrings from the other side of the dune. It seemed the mother had realized her most important whelp was still right where it needed be, and that was all that mattered to her. The hunt was a success... or so it would be, as soon as he found Klik and Bobo.

It was the duo who found him first, Bobo having risked taking to the air in the harsh winds to find Konta when he finally emerged. They both came up to him, cradling their shelled trophies who were still chomping away at the fruits, oblivious to the world. Bobo and Klik each managed to spare an arm to haul Konta to his feet and guide him as they trudged their way back to the dying forest.

It was only once they finally found some respite from the blasting heat and wind of the desert amongst some trees that they finally took a short rest. Bobo and Klik forced Konta to drink some extra munitions of water, against his wishes. They knew he needed the hydration, and with the victory of the Canteen Turtles, there would be no shortage of water for the tribe anytime soon.

* * *

Several hours later, the tribe had their three heroic hunters returned to them, a bit more bruised and battered than when they left, but still alive and lively. A small number of communal tents had been set up for the tribe to rest in before setting out again the next morning, and Bobo wasted no time in pulling himself into the nearest one for some well-deserved rest. Klik decided to take his reprieve near the fire while playing with his little boy Klikin, who seemed ready to burst with excitement at the return of his father.

Konta decided to watch the tribeswomen as they prepared the Canteen Turtles for the Summer to come. The beasts would not cooperate with them just because it was desired; there were certain measures that had to be taken to make sure they got what they wanted from their prizes.

How the Canteen Turtle did what it did was a mystery that was still unsolved by the tribesmen. Their unique physiology, whatever it was, allowed them to act as a sort of purification system: they could process anything they ate, regardless of toxicity or lack of nutrition, and turn it into sustenance for themselves. In the process, they extracted all moisture from what they ate, and as a result, the sole excretion that they voided from their bodies was water, pure and clean as any known. The oasis that the Canteen Turtles lived in on the mother Tortoasise's back was actually filled with this water, a byproduct of their remarkable bodies. With the two captured Turtles, the tribe had access to a steady supply of pure drinking water for the entire season, and all they had to do was feed the Turtles anything they had on hand. First, though, they had to prepare the Turtles for transport – this was a matter for the tribeswomen.

There was no denying the natural difference in the physiques of the men and women. The men developed larger, more powerful muscles than the women, and were, therefore, better suited to being trained in the hunt, as they had the best chance of striking lethal blows. However, many of the creatures that they hunted and fed upon – or in this case were captured and used as a tool – had to be specially prepared in order to get the full use out of it. This was what the tribeswomen did, and in contrast, their contribution to the tribe's well-being outweighed the men's by a considerable margin.

Konta sat and watched, spellbound by the grace and dexterity the women demonstrated as their expertly trained fingers ever so carefully measured out pinches and scrapes of various herbs, plants, and powders that had been foraged and stored for uses ranging from medicine to poison to spicing meals. Klik's wife, Klika, took these ingredients into a clay bowl and mixed them with a pestle, the concoction slowly being ground into a fine, bright orange powder.

A hand alighted on Konta's shoulder and he startled, looking up to see Kontala's brilliant eyes looking into his own. She gave a small, silent giggle at his reaction, something that only he would appreciate, especially after the struggle he had been through. With a weary smile, he tried to stand to hold her, but instead, she pushed him to the ground and wagged her finger at him, telling him to stay where he was.

With a surprising grace for someone bearing a child, she moved to the bowl and filled two small satchels with the powder. Inside each one she placed a straw made from a long, hollow blade of grass

49

and tied the satchels closed around them. Then she turned to where the two Canteen Turtles sat nearby, steadily being fed by a couple of younger tribeswomen who were being taught how to handle them by the village's eldest woman, whom Konta had given the name Marg.

Marg had once been the mate of Murg in her younger years. Now that she lacked the ability to have children and the pups she had were fully grown, she spent her remaining years teaching the younger girls how to handle the innumerable tasks that had to be done around the camp. It was that cohesion, everyone having their vital tasks that only they could do, that gave the tribe its unified strength to handle surviving in the harsh world they lived in.

So Konta watched as Marg mutely instructed the girls, showing them how to tilt the heads of the Turtles back without causing them to fight the forced movement, and how to hold them still while Kontala showed them how to insert the straws into the noses of the beasts so that they didn't resist. Once the straws were in, each girl plugged the uncovered nostril while Kontala quickly tipped both the satchels upwards, unloading their contents into the beasts' noses. The creatures stirred for a moment, but the effects of the powder were extremely fast acting when inhaled, and both Turtles instantly went stiff. They continued to grind their food in their mouths, but it was a lethargic, absent-minded chewing, as if their reflex wouldn't allow them to stop.

Now that they were subdued, the girls had no trouble affixing water catches made of strong, waterproof leaves and sap around the hindquarters of the Canteen Turtles. This way, they could be strapped to the back of a tribesman while the tribe wandered in search of a place they could set up camp for the season, and the water they produced on the way would be collected until it could be better stored in a sturdier container.

Their job finally done, the young girls were dismissed. Sweat beaded on their brows from their concentration but their faces were alight with their newfound knowledge. Marg set about to finding a place for the Canteen Turtles to be kept safe that night. Her wizened body, forged strong from hundreds of seasons of backbreaking labor, had little trouble handling the large beasts as she relocated them to a more discreet location. Konta wanted to help, but the trials of the day had left him drained of strength.

Kontala floated down beside him, as if sensing his weariness, and rested her head on his shoulder just as she had during their last Settling. Her hand rested on his chest, telling him that his exhaustion was well earned, and that he needn't move until he was ready. After how many times he had cheated death that day, with Kontala and his young progeny resting here beside him, he felt like he would've liked to stay where he was, in that moment, until he drew his last breath.

The Cactyringe

Konta was awakened one stiflingly hot morning by two sharp taps on the shoulder. Today was supposed to be a day of rest for him while the other hunters of the tribe were out foraging, and he had decided to sleep just slightly later than usual. To be woken up by a fellow tribesman was sure to mean that something was wrong.

He turned to find his mate, Kontala, kneeling beside him. One look at her heat-flushed face and Konta could tell that something was amiss. Her eyes were wide and impatient, and before Konta could try and figure out what was going on, she had already started dragging him to his feet. He put a reassuring hand on her own before pulling her grip from him. No matter the urgency of the situation, he couldn't run out into the intensity of the Summer Sun without a scrap of clothing on. It only took moments for Konta to wrap himself from head to toe in thick robes, leaving only a small space open on his face to see out of.

He emerged from his tepee into the stifling heat of Summer, which had descended upon the tribe with full force. They had managed to see the warning signs early enough to take necessary precautions for their safety, but there was no such thing as a gentle Summer. Even with a pair of Canteen Turtles supplying the tribe with fresh water, they had to find an area to settle in that would provide a modicum of shelter from the incessant sandstorms and unbearable heat that would attack them each day.

Fortunately, the tribe had found a depression in the sand dunes surrounded by several large boulders. The area was shaded against the Sun during several points in the day, and the natural bowl shape of the area allowed it to capture heat, making the bitter-cold night much more bearable. It was as ideal a place as they could hope to find to set up camp until Summer had passed.

Now Konta struggled against the sand whipped into his face by the wind that managed to squeeze between the rocks, trying to find where Kontala had gone to. He saw a heavily cloaked figure waving at him from a distance, its belly slightly distended, and noticed with a twang of dread that Kontala was standing in front of the medicinal tent. Someone was either hurt or sick.

Passing through the curtain into the tent, he saw Kontala and Marg, the elderly medicine woman, standing over a child currently lying on a rug. The young girl he recognized as Grimzi, daughter of tribeswoman Grima and her mate Grim. She was clutching at her arm and whimpering, her brow covered with a damp cloth. Konta marched forward and knelt beside the girl, removing the cloth to feel her forehead – she was burning with fever. He gently pulled Grimzi's hand away from her arm, where he saw a large welt, the skin around it discolored a grotesque purple. He knew the signs right away of Desert Flower poisoning.

The Desert Flower was no plant by any means, but rather a highly toxic species of scorpion. It took the shape of a brightly colored flower in order to lure in unsuspecting prey before striking it with one of several dozen "petals" surrounding its body, which were, in fact, a multitude of stingers. The stinger detached from the scorpion once used, continuing to inject poison into the victim until removed. A Desert Flower's stingers never regrew, but the sheer number of stingers it possessed made it a terrible threat throughout its lifespan nonetheless. The girl most likely was playing alone and came across the creature, its camouflage tricking the unsuspecting child all too well.

Marg had already removed the stinger, but the poison of the Desert Flower was quite powerful even in small doses. For such a small child, it was incredible that she was still alive at all. Undoubtedly, Marg had already given her some antitoxin, but from the look of the wound, Konta could see that it wasn't enough to nullify the poison.

Marg had retrieved one of the pictograph books they kept with the medical supplies to diagnose ailments and record their various cures and set it before Konta. The page, made from the dried hide of some beast, was open to a picture of the very condition they now beheld: a picture of a discolored wound, a large inflammation in the center, with a drawing of the Desert Flower beside it. On the next page was a picture of the only known cure for the toxin, a large green plant with stocky branches and countless needles, a couple of flowers blooming randomly on its trunk – the Cactyringe.

The Cactyringe was one of the only plants adapted to the harsh environs of Summer, capable of drawing what little water possible from the dry sand and soil. Its many needles thwarted attempts creatures made to eat it, and while the flowers that bloomed on its surface were a great source of nutrition, they were also almost identical to the Desert Flower in appearance, which naturally made the Cactyringe a desirable nesting area for the deceptive scorpions.

Konta knew that the antidote for the Desert Flower's toxin was produced from the Cactyringe, and with all the other hunters gone from the camp, he knew it was on his shoulders to procure what they needed to produce more antitoxin before the girl succumbed. However, there was another problem to surmount besides the ones already presented to them. Konta, being a hunter strictly, was not knowledgeable in how exactly to obtain what they needed from the Cactyringe to create the antidote they needed. That area of expertise was the domain of the tribeswomen.

No sooner had he thought it, Konta turned to see his mate pulling another woman into the tent. It was Klika, wife of Konta's fellow hunter Klik, and one of the tribeswomen who was more experienced in medical remedies. Konta watched as Klika rushed to the child and examined her at a glance, taking note of the book still open to the diagnosis. Within moments Klika had gotten a grasp on the situation and stood ready to do whatever necessary to save the young girl's life. Marg pointed swiftly to Konta and Klika and then motioned to the book. Her message was quite clear: Konta needed to help Klika find the Cactyringe so that she may gather what they needed to treat the injury.

It wasn't unheard of for a hunter to escort a tribeswoman on a hunt for a particular ingredient, but it was a rare occurrence; normally, anything needed for the tribe's well-being would be found by hunters alone, brought back to the village, and prepared in the safety of the community by the tribeswomen there. The only time tribeswomen headed into the field with hunters was when the ingredient in question was difficult or impossible to procure without special preparation. The Cactyringe seemed to be just such a case, and so it was upon Konta to protect the medicine woman and deliver her safely to their quarry. With time being of the essence, Konta wasted none of it as he left the tent in all haste, Klika following right behind him.

Cactyringes were not difficult to find, for the most part, as they weren't a plant that required special circumstances to grow, and they tended to grow in large numbers. As Konta stood on the rocky outcropping that overlooked the tribe's encampment, he contemplated which direction they needed to head in to find their prey. He knew that the Desert Flower was a creature that didn't stray far from its nesting grounds, preferring instead to wait for prey to approach it – therefore, there had to be a Cactyringe grove somewhere close by. Noting that he couldn't see a grove from where he stood, Konta figured that perhaps the strong winds had blown the Desert Flower nearby, in which case their best bet in finding a Cactyringe quickly was to head against the desert gales. With a curt hand gesture, he pointed Klika to the west and set off at a brisk pace.

At the top of the first dune, Konta squinted through the blasting sands to get bearings. Off to their right in the distance, he could make out the shape of a glittering blue lake, a couple of palm trees bearing large orange fruit dotting the banks. A grim smirk crossed his face for but an instant, glad that his prey this time was something far less harrowing, and he returned to the task at hand. Directly in front of the duo was a large flat wasteland, without another dune to be seen for miles. A large number of identical, branching shapes sprouted from the ground in a close cluster, and Konta sighed a breath of relief – their target was right in sight. Klika had seen the shapes too, and didn't hesitate to take the lead as she marched down the slope with Konta in tow.

Konta's relief was short-lived as the Cactyringe grove grew closer, and apprehension began to set upon him. The Cactyringe itself was not much of a threat, as long as one was careful to avoid the razor-sharp needles as long as a man's finger that covered the plants from top to bottom. What the real danger came from was the creature that made Cactyringe groves its hunting grounds and nests, the creature that started this whole hunt: the Desert Flower.

Konta's experience with the Desert Flower was well ingrained in his training as a hunter. It was considered one of the greatest threats during the months of Summer, and Konta had lost more than one friend in his childhood to this deceptive arachnid. The hunters that had trained him when he was but a pup had taken him and those his age to a Cactyringe grove shortly after the third Desert Flower attack one Summer, and they showed the pups how to tell the scorpion apart from the flowers that naturally grew on the Cactyringe. It was not an easy task, but there was an important reason to make the distinction: the Cactyringe plants that could be used to create the Desert Flower antitoxin never had a nest within them. Konta now had to use that knowledge to find a plant that they could use to obtain what they needed.

He realized with a start that, as he was absorbed in thought, Klika had rushed towards the nearest Cactyringe, removing a small, precise knife with which to prepare the plant. In a flash of movement, Konta removed the small flint knife he had tucked in his waistcloth, and with the swiftest of motions, stabbed a flower that had been crawling ever so patiently towards Klika's outstretched hand. He grabbed her around her shoulders and pulled her back forcefully as several other Desert Flowers crawled from their resting places, their petal-like stingers twitching eagerly at the sign of prey. Konta gave Klika a pointed look before grabbing her hand and, to her apparent astonishment, led her directly into the grove.

Konta knew that as long as they didn't stray too close to a nested Cactyringe, they had little fear of a surprise attack, and any suspicious flower on the ground could be easily avoided; Desert Flowers were notoriously slow moving hunters. Konta walked between the succulent plants, carefully winding through them in an effort to find the widest path available. More than once, one of the long needles would catch on his robe, and the sudden vibration would send the Desert Flowers nesting on the plant to rush forward as fast as they could, tails quivering expectantly. Still, his experience allowed him to keep well outside their striking range, and with a quick tug, he'd free himself. Klika, being led by hand, was free to keep her attention on making sure her own wraps didn't catch in a similar fashion.

Their search range was limited to the edge of the immense grove, in case a hasty retreat became necessary, but it didn't take more than a few tense minutes for Konta to stop in front of a Cactyringe that didn't particularly stand out from the others. He leaned in as close as he dared, taking careful note of the flowers. The distinguishing characteristic between the Desert Flower and the flowers that grew on the Cactyringe was the thin, transparent stinger that tipped every "petal" of the scorpion. While normally very difficult to see with the naked eye, these stingers glinted in a very peculiar manner when viewed just right in the sunlight. With the Cactyringe grove blocking the majority of the sandstorms and the Sun high overhead, it took little effort for Konta's well-trained eye to see these stingers.

The flower he now examined had no indication of such stingers, so he took a slight stab at it with his knife. It quivered slightly from the strike, but otherwise did not stir. He made eye contact with Klika and nodded towards the Cactyringe, indicating it was safe. Klika was still hesitant to approach, now that she had a better understanding of the dangers at hand, but at Konta's silent insistence, she finally pulled out her small knife again and set to work, now comfortable dealing with her subject.

Konta watched on, amazed, as she carefully shaved off several of the deadly needles, isolating a thorn that, upon close inspection, appeared longer and thicker than the others. Ever so carefully, with fingers trained in dealing with the most delicate subjects, Klika cut into the thick flesh of the Cactyringe, slicing slowly around her selected needle. Once she cut full circle, she gingerly pinched the needle at the base and the tip, and with a continuous, measured pull that seemed to last ages they couldn't spare, she pulled the segment free.

Konta's eyes grew wide as he saw what lay on the other side of the chunk of plant she removed. A large, bulbous pod quivered on the back end, undulating slightly even now as she held it. Konta could hear a slight sloshing from within the pod, indicating it was brimming with some sort of fluid. Without hesitation she wrapped the needle and the pod carefully in a thick cloth and placed it in her satchel. She looked at Konta and nodded poignantly, indicating that they had what they needed, and without a second thought, Konta led them back through the grove.

Finally free of the deadly plants, Konta took off at a sprint towards the village, but slowed quickly when he noticed that Klika was lagging far behind. She was taking great care to coddle the satchel that held their prize, and Konta realized that with her precious cargo, she couldn't move too quickly, lest the ingredient be damaged and their effort be for naught. Still, he knew that every second could prove fatal to the girl, so in an act of desperate thinking, he rushed back to her and lifted the tribeswoman into his arms, cradling her as he would a child. He stood still for only a moment, hoping she would follow his line of thought, and after her initial shock, she seemed to understand what he was trying to do, and carefully cradled the package against her chest. She was entrusting the final stretch to Konta's area of expertise.

With a mad burst of adrenaline, Konta took off, unhindered by Klika's weight. Having been required to run while encumbered from predators innumerable times in his life, Konta was more than accustomed to the strain and made much better time than Klika would've while trying to run and protect the parcel at the same time. He sprinted onward, devoted to his purpose, while she focused on keeping the ingredient intact, and together their efforts got them back to camp before the Sun had crept any further in the sky, their cargo completely unharmed.

They had arrived not a moment too soon, as Konta observed in further amazement how their hunt had procured not just a remedy for the scorpion's toxin, but a method of application. Klika wasted no time inserting the Cactyringe's needle directly into the child's inflammation. The bulb on the back of the needle pulsed madly, and through the thin, partially transparent needle, Konta could see a purplish liquid being discharged through the needlepoint and into the girl's arm.

Results were almost instantaneous as the swollen area began to reduce in size, the discoloration faded slightly, and the girl's ragged breathing grew normal as she fell into a peaceful sleep. It made Konta wonder, ever so slightly, how the Cactyringe could produce such an incredible cure without any human preparation. Did it use the needle as protection from being destroyed by the Desert Flowers nesting around it? If so, what causes only certain Cactyringes to be protected from the scorpions that live freely in other hosts?

At the end of the day, it didn't matter. A precious member of their tribe had been saved, and a small communal gathering was held that night to commemorate Konta and Klika's swift action in the face of adversity. Konta sat with Kontala, sipping contently on a fermented drink, and as Grimzi approached him and gave him a small bracelet she wove from flowers, he was happy to be reaffirmed that his skill as a hunter could do more than just take life.

The Sand Eye

The Sand Bee

Summer seemed to drag on almost uneventfully for Konta and his tribe after the Desert Flower incident, as the revolution of the Sun and Moon marked days that turned into weeks. The occasional sandstorm was the greatest threat that attacked the nomads, but it was something they had lived through for many Summers, and they plowed through it with their usual stubbornness. The hunters were able to secure food from sources such as the flightless Dunerunner bird and the reclusive Funnel Mole, both of which were less dangerous than the average beasts that roamed during the season. Still, the tribe was always vigilant for those deceptive Summer animals that they had already encountered more than they would've liked.

It was during one Summer morning, as Konta was just waking and going about his daily preparations alongside the tribeswomen, that a scout returned from his rounds out of breath and looking rather ragged. The scout, a fairly new recruit to their night-time fold whom Konta knew as Tamto, had something clutched tightly in his hand and rushed to the chief's tent without acknowledging any other tribesmen. This naturally drew the attention of everyone nearby, and they rushed to see what he had to show the chief so urgently.

Murg was just stirring from sleep, slipping on his crude loincloth as Tamto burst in. Still flushed and panting, the scout extended his hand and showed its contents to the chief. Immediately, Murg went pale, his eyes narrowing at the sight of whatever it was. His brow furrowed for a moment, and then he turned and began to roll things up and pack them.

The crowd of people who waited at the mouth of the tent scrambled to see what the chief had just seen, but they didn't have long to wait. As Tamto turned, his eyes wide and his pallid face livid with terror, he displayed the object he had retrieved during his night hunting – an object that immediately caused most of the witnesses to back away, their mouths silently agape in fear.

It was a long, thin barb that closely resembled a dagger, its material translucent and tinged the color of sand. At the wider end, what appeared to be ragged, dried flesh still clung loosely to the object. Konta knew there was no denying that this object was the stinger from a molting Sand Bee.

Sand Bees were a far too common occurrence during Summer, vicious creatures that were – like humans – mostly nomadic in nature. They wandered from area to area, braving the sandstorms and blistering heats to find suitable nesting grounds. Once they found a place they deemed suitable, they would burrow intricate hives in the sands and lay their eggs. After their job was done, the entire swarm would die, but their egg clusters would continue to grow, safe from the relentless seasons in their expertly made nests, until next Summer came around, at which time the new swarm would hatch and emerge, feeding endlessly and growing at a frightening pace until they too found a new nesting site, and the process would repeat.

This stinger was a sign that a Sand Bee had just recently molted and was within range of the campsite. If it possessed such a dangerous stinger before molting, Konta knew that it likely had one twice the size by now, and there was an entire swarm possibly converging on the camp at this moment.

Without an instant's hesitation, the tribe exploded into a flurry of movement as the rest of the tribe was woken, everyone hurrying to take down whatever they could and pack it as quickly as possible. Some things would have to be left behind. The risk of being attacked by a swarm of Sand Bees was far more pressing than saving something as replaceable as a hide tent.

Once everyone had loaded up the bare essentials and covered themselves as needed, the tribe was off, going the opposite direction from where Tamto had found the barb. Fortunately, all the scouts had returned before they departed. There was no time to wait for stragglers with such a threat descending upon the tribe.

Summer felt no sympathy for their plight, and the winds seemed to only increase in intensity as the tribe rose from the depression they had been camping in those last few months. Sand buffeted them relentlessly as they tried their best to forge forwards, the storm blowing directly into them as if to deliberately impede their progress. The stoutest warriors took the lead, doing their best to absorb the brunt of the force and make things even the slightest bit easier for the women and children to move onward. The other hunters stayed on the outer perimeter to defend against anything, Sand Bee or otherwise, that might spring a trap upon their very vulnerable group.

Attacks were only one plight the group faced. They had been forced from a very advantageous location so suddenly that the tribe was not quite sure where they should go next. The scouts had not found any similar camping sites in the range of their hunting grounds, so the only choice they had was to forge onward and hope that they would happen upon some place they could set up camp for at least a short time.

Konta was walking near the back of the troupe, looking half-passively from one tribesman to another, his hand on the shoulder of Kontala who walked just ahead of him. As he struggled to keep a close eye on everyone and make sure nobody was separated, there came through the air a noise that immediately caught Konta's attention. Despite the howling winds, there was no mistaking that there was something else out there, making a high-pitched buzzing that cut through the desert maelstrom and caused Konta's very bones to rattle.

The first one materialized as if from nowhere, bursting through the sand curtain from the group's right with stinger poised menacingly. Zanzu, though he was one of the hunters covering the front, immediately lunged from his position, pulling the massive spear he carved himself from his back and impaling the attacker in one swift motion. The creature twitched spasmodically at the end of the spit for but a moment before it went still. Konta could barely see it even from his vantage point, for its carapace was a perfect match for the sand and dust that billowed about the group. Its compound eyes, however, reflected the cruel light of the Sun readily enough, void and emotionless.

The buzzing now reached a fierce intensity, and immediately the tribeswomen and children threw themselves to the ground to try and protect themselves. The hunters had all unsheathed their spears, encircling the huddled group while facing outwards to deflect any incoming attack. The chances of fighting off an entire swarm of Sand Bees was nigh impossible, but the tribe had one boon that could possibly save them at this juncture.

Konta spared a glance towards Klik, who was the only hunter who had yet to draw his spear. Instead, he was furiously uncovering his pelt, which was among the most delicate of all the hunters' cloaks and thus was usually tucked away during the day, when the harsh Summer storms could damage it. That cloak was the only hope the tribe had of getting out of this situation, and it was up to the other hunters to fend off their attackers until Klik was ready.

Within moments, another half-dozen Bees dove on the tribe, their deadly barbs unfurling from within their bodies and pointed straight at the hunters. The spears of the hunters were thankfully just long enough to strike at the Sand Bees from outside their range. The real danger was in missing. As fast and agile as the Sand Bees were, a single failed strike would give them enough time to attack, and Konta knew the Sand Bees wouldn't miss their mark.

Before the last of the new attackers had fallen, another dozen emerged to attack. Konta was able to strike one down with a single blow, but found it lodged firmly on the head of the spear. As he tried to kick it off the end, a Sand Bee appeared from the storm right in front of him. With the stinger just an arm's length from him, he instinctively turned his back it.

The attack glanced off the rock-hard fur of his Obsidian Panther pelt, and as the beast fell to the ground from the sudden recoil, Konta wheeled around and drove the spear straight down. The fire-hardened point burst through the Sand Bee stuck to the end and impaled the one that had just attacked him.

As the hunters fought desperately to keep their attackers at bay, Konta noticed that the sandstorm was beginning to abate. Thoughts that some good fortune had befallen them were quickly replaced with horrible realization as he saw the massive shadow that blotted out the Sun above their heads. The hunters looked up, and now it was clear that the storm's subsiding was caused by the rapid wing fluttering of what appeared to be over a hundred Sand Bees hovering just above their group.

Konta's stomach felt as if it had sunk to his knees, unable to conceive how they could stop the next attack, when through the air there came a high pitched whistling that rang so sharply Konta couldn't help but put his hands to his ears. The rest of the tribe followed suit, looking pointedly in the direction this new sound emanated from.

A figure was now stepping out from amid the ring of hunters, clad in a cloak that shimmered in the weak sunlight with every color imaginable, the brilliant hues changing like an aurora as they skimmed across the carapace. Its eyes shone even brighter, the lights dancing across their hexed surfaces in complex patterns, and its transparent wings were flapping at a dizzying pace, acting almost like prisms as the reflected light from the hide glanced through them and scattered the colors in a dazzling array. Konta felt a new surge of hope as Klik slowly advanced towards the tremendous horde that was now visibly shirking away.

While Sand Bees were one of the great terrible hunters of Summer, there was a predator that alone could drive away even an entire swarm of Sand Bees – their natural enemy, the Wonderwasp. The creature's appearance was always heralded by the loud buzzing they now heard, an almost hypnotic noise that, combined with the brilliant rainbow array they displayed in the Sun, was mesmerizing to any creature that beheld it. They were by far considered the most fearsome creature of Summer, but so rare was their appearance that they would almost be considered myth, if it weren't for Klik's possession of one's carapace.

He had come into acquisition of it some years ago, returning in the dead of night with its lifeless body. The tribeswomen, in their incredible ingenuity, were able to rig the delicate membrane wings it possessed so they could be made to vibrate by pulling a cord hidden within the folds of the cowl, but the wings were so fragile even when cured that Klik had to keep them well folded within the cloak during Summer, lest the vicious winds rip them apart.

Now he had donned this same cloak, the carapace perfectly replicating the astonishing light refraction it bore in life, the wings still able to create that spellbinding buzz that caused the Sand Bees to back away immediately. So great was the Sand Bee's instinctual fear of the Wonderwasp, that no sooner did Klik begin to advance on them with his cloak on than the entire swarm lifted as one, retreating the same direction the tribe had just been retreating from. Klik continued to make the cloak's wings beat furiously, drowning out the howling winds with his terrifying buzz for several minutes before finally relenting as the sandstorm picked up strength again. He hastily stowed away his cloak lest it get damaged from prolonged exposure, but it had appeared to have done its job – there was not so much as a gentle hum in the air anymore.

The tribe gave a collective sigh of relief, and Murg and Zanzu quickly gathered a headcount to make sure everyone was accounted for. Last time the tribe had been attacked by Sand Bees – a time that was before Klik had acquired his incredible cowl – three of their fold had been taken before the creatures could be driven off by fire. It seemed that everyone had managed through the ordeal safely enough, save for a few less seasoned hunters who had been suffered minor cuts or punctures from the Sand Bees' stingers. Fortunately, antitoxin for Sand Bee venom was easily procured, and they were treated before any ill effects befell them. They had fought the catastrophic odds and come out with little more than flesh wounds, a best-case scenario indeed.

They didn't dare spend any more time than necessary where they were, lest the Sand Bees come back for them again, and quickly retreated in a different direction, hoping to throw their possible pursuers off their trail. Night fell before they had found a new shelter from the harsh sandstorms. With nightfall also came a calming to the winds, and the tribe decided to simply set up camp in a small impression between several dunes for the night.

While they had lost their haven from the storms of Summer, the tribe was ecstatic at their narrow escape from the terrible clutches of the Sand Bees. There was a small celebration that night to commemorate Klik, whose expertise as a hunter had saved the tribe from what could have been a very sobering ordeal. At the same time, they celebrated one of the lesser hunters who had killed his first beast single-handedly in the attack.

Konta never thought of names for hunters who had yet to kill their first prey, and though he named the young of other hunters, this boy's parents had died before Konta had become accustomed to his method of naming, so this hunter had simply passed by his notice until this moment. Now, as the tribe celebrated his first kill, Konta recognized him as a full-fledged asset to the tribe, thinking of him as Senga. When the tribe settled again, the tribeswomen would set to curing the carcass of the Sand Bee he had brought back with him, creating a cowl of his own he could wear proudly on his hunts.

Though the day had been harrowing, it was simply a grim reminder for Konta that there was no place that was safe for them in this world. He watched Kontala, smiling serenely as she watched the new Senga dance joyously around the fire with Klik, her hand resting gently on her belly that was now larger than Konta's head, and wondered what kind of child he would come to raise. Would it be a boy, who would one day grow to be a strong young hunter like Senga, or would it be a girl who would eventually learn the intricate arts of medicine and anatomy that were indispensable to the tribe's continuation, perhaps one day creating a pelt like that of the Wonderwasp that the entire tribe's safety could rely on?

He strode to Kontala, knelt down, and put his arms around her, burying his face in her soft, wild hair. The only thing he wished for at that moment was the strength to protect his cub so that they could one day fulfill their given destiny, no matter what that would be.

The Weeping Willow

Summer was finally ending. This was the foremost thought on Konta's weary mind as his tribe was slowly preparing to get on the move once more. They had managed to make it to the valley they usually camped in during the arduous Summer months, a veritable haven compared to most other choices – high walls blocked the Sun during the day and trapped heat in at night, the narrow valley discouraged most larger predators from coming in, and the bedrock that floored the area protected from any unwanted visitors underfoot. It was the perfect place to rest and recuperate after the harrowing attack from the Sand Bees, but Konta knew this would be short-lived. The other day, he caught sight of the first wisp of cloud, which was a telltale sign of Autumn's coming.

While the Summer and Winter Solstices were the most unforgiving seasonal changes and their end was normally considered a great relief, there was always

75

a new set of challenges that had to be addressed with any season's arrival. In the case of Autumn, Konta's tribe had to be very careful not to be caught in the valley they camped in when the Equinox hit in full force. Otherwise, this place of refuge would quickly become a grave for their people.

Everything was in order, the village now placed literally on the backs of the young fledgling hunters as the tribe began to migrate once more to find a place to set up for the coming season. The skies overhead had already begun to darken with great black clouds; by tomorrow, the heat they had just been enduring would be nothing more than a vague memory.

Konta marched besides his dear Kontala, whose belly had grown so large that she now had difficulty walking. They had to move quickly to get out of the valley before the first rains fell, but with a woman bearing child in the group, the tribe had to make sure to take frequent short rests so as to not overexert her. When a child was expected in the tribe, its safe deliverance was one of the foremost thoughts taken when handling a relocation, and Kontala was no exception.

Even with the periodic stops, the tribe made good time as their path began to widen and slope upwards. The Sun was only just beginning to dip below the horizon, but they could not stop to set up camp for the night until they had gotten well clear of the path they currently traveled. The incline was too strenuous for Kontala to walk, and so she had to be carried the last leg of the trek on a stretcher the tribeswomen had strung together from the plants that had begun to grow in expectation of Autumn. Held aloft by Konta and Faygo, Konta's friend and fellow hunter, everyone was able to hasten their pace, and before long they noticed the walls becoming shorter with each passing step, finally reaching the top of the canyon before the Sun had fully set.

The tribe had entered into a deep indentation in the land that was surrounded by lush green vegetation, a sight Konta hadn't seen in months. Nature had already anticipated the end of Summer's brutal heat, and the plants were out in full force, eagerly awaiting Autumn's bounty. He knew that by tonight, those plants would receive their wish, but for now the tribe had to make sure they were well clear of the valley and that indentation before setting up for the night. It was only after they had traveled far enough to completely lose sight of these that they finally lay down their bedrolls to rest.

While the women and children prepared to sleep, the hunters were busy erecting tarps over a large area that would cover the entire tribe. These tarps were the same ones they used during Spring to keep the occasional rain off, woven from the leaves of the Weeping Willow and held strong by the tree's caulking sap. Konta knew that tonight, though, these tarps would be far more important than they were that last time.

Not a single hunter was allowed to sleep that night. The scouts had been sent out to look for a better place to set up camp when the tribe awoke in the morning, but the rest of the hunters had to be on constant alert to protect the village while they lay out in the open unprotected.

As Konta sat at the edge of the tarp, staring out over the inky blackness with his trusted hammer in hand, there was a sudden flash of light as the sky seemed to crack for the briefest of moments. He knew what was coming, and sure enough, a few seconds later there came an incredible crashing sound that shook the night. He felt Kontala's clutch as she grabbed at his pelt; undoubtedly, she had been startled awake from the noise. Konta turned and laid a reassuring hand on her shoulder, noticing that most of the women and children had been stirred awake from the thunder. Only the eldest of the women, having experienced this for innumerable rotations of the seasons, did not rise from their slumber.

As the tribe tried to settle back to sleep, the first pattering of raindrops could be heard overhead. The soft, soothing rhythm aided the tribeswomen and children as they did their best to rest, but Konta and the other hunters grew intensely alert at this. Autumn was upon them completely now: a season of unending rain where predators could hide practically in the open and never be seen. Tonight, it was every hunter's job to watch out for those beasts that were surely now crawling out from their Summer hibernation, preparing to revel in this cascading curtain.

Konta loved the rain. The way it sounded as it hit the ground, the shifting patterns it wove through the sky as it fell, these were all things that left him spellbound as he sat at the edge of the temporary camp, staring out into the darkness that was only broken by the occasional lightning strike. However, the very things that made him love the rain also made him terrified of it. He had to be careful not to be too distracted, for all it took was a single moment's lapse in concentration for a predator to make him its next meal.

There were a couple tense moments during the night when an unusual sound would draw the attention of the hunters, but nothing ever came of these small outbursts. Konta assumed that these noises were the aftermath of some unknown creature succeeding in their first hunt of the season.

Konta's nerves were stretched to the breaking point by the time morning finally rose, though now the sky was so thick with clouds that the difference between day and night was minimal at best. Within the hour of "Sunrise," the scouts had all returned. Most simply shook their heads as Murg approached them, looking for information, but it seemed that one had perhaps found a promising lead.

Bobo was looking slightly agitated, and Konta noticed a bandage wrapped tightly around his arm that hadn't been present the night before, the cloth tinged slightly red. When Murg approached him, Bobo tapped the tarp overhead with his finger, then cupped his hands together and pulled them apart, wincing from the pain of moving his injured arm. Murg understood what Bobo was signifying, and quickly tapped him on the chest. Murg then wandered along the ring of hunters that had been keeping watch, giving a short tap on the chest of a choice few of them as he looked them over, Konta included.

It was going to be a rough job for Konta, who was already weary with fatigue, but he knew he'd have to tough it out so he could help secure a suitable camping site for the tribe. Aside from himself, Konta noted that the chief had selected Zanzu, Faygo, and an older hunter named Bren for the hunt. From what Konta could tell, Murg had chosen the hunters who looked the most lively after their all-night vigil, and despite how tired Konta felt, he could tell there were other hunters who were far worse off.

It only took a few minutes for the group to get their choice weapons together and head out, following Bobo's lead as he made his way to his discovery. Travel was painfully slow, as they had to be extra cautious moving through the heavy rain so as to not arouse the curiosity of Autumn predators. Fortunately, the rain helped conceal them as much as their foes, washing away their footprints and any telltale signs they might have left behind otherwise.

Konta already had a good idea of the camping ground Bobo had found for the tribe, and his suspicions were confirmed as a large form loomed ahead, obscured by the rain. As the hunting party drew closer, the great shape of a tree began to manifest before them, its branches and drooping leaves billowing out to create a sort of umbrella shape that extended well beyond the base of the trunk. It was a tree that the tribe was well familiar with, for the tribe had used its resources several times before to create a myriad of useful tools, not the least of which was the tarp they had been camping under just hours earlier.

The Weeping Willow was not a rare tree by any means, with entire groves of them often appearing during Autumn when the tree could make full use of the abundance of water available. Its leaves were thin but strong, coated with a waxy resin that acted as a natural sealant, making the leaves virtually waterproof, and the tree's sap was employed by the tribe often as a binding agent for various uses. The widespread blooming shape of the branches, combined with the Willow's inherent watertight biology, made it the perfect haven to wait out the endless downpour of Autumn.

Of course, all these boons came with a heavy trade-off. Konta knew that other creatures instinctively sought out these trees as nesting areas during Autumn, which acted not only as shelter for any beast that made its home there, but as the perfect trap for unsuspecting prey. Predators could safely wait high in the thick canopy of the Willow, completely hidden, and wait for a hapless victim to seek refuge from the rain under the tree.

These trees were so desirable as shelter that it was assumed by the tribe that any and every Weeping Willow they came across was already inhabited, and therefore dangerous to venture near. An entire grove of them was considered the same as an entire village of hungry predators just waiting for them. However, a lone Weeping Willow would be a great place to camp, as their shape would make it easy to detect approaching predators and chase them off, in addition to the obvious cover from the rain it afforded.

So, it fell on Konta and this hunting party to evict any predators that may have holed up in what was otherwise a perfect camping spot. The real danger didn't come from the fact that there likely *were* predators in the tree, though, as much as it came from the uncertainty of what exactly was currently waiting for them. There were several creatures well known for making the Willow their choice nesting area, and approaching haphazardly would be a death sentence for the party.

The Willow finally came into clear view as they reached the edge of the branches, and now Konta and his fellow hunters knew clearly what they were about to face. The tree had been covered with blood, the deep crimson liquid made runny by the rain as it cascaded down the leaves and splattered the ground, creating a visible ring around the entirety of the Weeping Willow.

The name Konta had chosen for this particular tree was derived from the phenomenon he now beheld, an image of a tree crying tears of blood that had been burned into his mind at a young age when he was still training to become a hunter. The first Willow he had ever seen had borne these markings, a territorial warning sign of beasts that Konta knew as Ravagers.

He had seen only a corpse of one before – a beast that appeared to look like a small, grotesque child with gnarled hands, needle-like teeth, and opposable thumbs on its feet – and had decided that the creature must have been communal in nature, for it seemed far too small to be a threat by itself. Konta's namesake for them came from the savage and ruthless displays they made to ward off predators. Konta had learned long ago that during Autumn, when Ravagers hunted to store food for the coming Winter, they would make their homes in a Weeping Willow as quickly as possible in order to take advantage of the cover it provided from both the rain and from other foes more dangerous than they. As an added precaution, Ravagers would gather the blood from the prey they caught and douse the tree in it, marking their territory and scaring away potential enemies.

Despite the information he had gleaned throughout the seasons, he still had little idea of what they were capable of when alive, since the last time he had seen a Weeping Willow marked so he was too young to accompany the hunters in their extermination. Konta wasn't sure what to expect, but Zanzu showed no hesitancy as he crossed over the bloodied boundary line. Bren was close on his heels, having lived long enough to have likely encountered a Ravager before. Bobo was injured and exhausted from a night of scouting, so he had taken up hiding nearby so that he could quickly return to the rest of the tribe when their mission was done, or if things turned ugly. Though Faygo and Konta had yet to hunt a Ravager before, they wasted no time in following their elders in. Konta hoped that the boldness Zanzu and Bren exhumed was an indication of their confidence in being able to set about this task.

It seemed that day turned to night in an instant as Konta entered the undergrowth of the Willow. The thickness of the foliage was unnerving to him, for even after his eyes adjusted to the lack of light he couldn't see anything moving in the thick of the branches overhead. The ground was muddy and reeked of blood, and though he couldn't be certain in the darkness, Konta was fairly sure he could make out several shapeless lumps around the base of the trunk: undoubtedly the remains of the Ravagers' last meals.

The sound of the rain had been muffled by the thick canopy, but that silence was broken quickly as a shrill cry rang out just in front of Konta. Something had dropped on Zanzu's back, and thus had the misfortune of landing directly on the arm's length blades that made up Zanzu's Razorback Mammoth pelt. The poor beast writhed around in agony, which only caused it to lacerate itself further before finally succumbing to its wounds.

The branches overhead began to shake, and Konta was just barely able to leap out of the way as several more Ravagers landed where he had been only seconds ago. Before they could regain their composure, Konta brought his great hammer round and swung it square into the middle of the bunch. He could feel as the force of the hammer's weight plowed through the tight knit group, the sound of snapping bones filling him with a rush of adrenaline.

He could hear the angry cries of the Ravagers all around him, but Konta knew at this point that numbers were just about the only advantage these creatures had. The three or four he had smashed with the hammer hadn't so much as twitched after their brief exchange. As another fell down only to be sidestepped and subsequently pummeled with Konta's special weapon, his confidence began to well up as he actively looked around for new targets to tackle.

Zanzu and Bren were having little trouble with their assailants, as Bren efficiently struck down one Ravager after another with his spear and Zanzu simply ripped them apart with his bare hands. Konta was half-musing which were more vicious between Zanzu and the Ravagers when there rose a great yelp that was all too distinct: a human cry.

Faygo had been pounced on by a lone Ravager, which clasped onto his neck with its hand-like feet and was raining blows down with its free arms. The attacks didn't seem to hurt Faygo much, but as he struggled to pull the Ravager off, about half a dozen more saw this moment of weakness and instantly focused their attention on him, leeching on and biting or clawing with their long dirty nails savagely. Even as he shouted out in dismay, Faygo reached to the mouth of his pelt and pulled the jaw of it down.

Konta had been present on the hunt for the Triceraboar that Faygo killed to get his pelt. While the piggish beast was large and muscular, its most prominent defense mechanism was a set of three bony spikes on its head that, at a glance, appear to be horns. It was only after the creature was killed and brought back to the tribe that they discovered that these horns were actually three long fangs that protruded through its skull- one near the front of its mouth that went through its nose, with the other two situated near the back of its mouth that emerged from atop its skull. This strange property gave a number of advantages for the creature, for by keeping its mouth closed it could gore prey on its snout, and by unhinging its jaw and opening wide it could extend the rear teeth from its crown suddenly for a deathblow.

This property had been preserved when the tribeswomen crafted the Triceraboar into a pelt for Faygo, and now the great fangs of the beast shot out from near his shoulders, striking and killing two Ravagers that had just been clamoring on top of him. Zanzu had already seen Faygo's distress and strode over in two steps, using his absurdly strong fingers to pry away the firm grip of the beasts, breaking their fingers in the process. Even injured as he was, Faygo wasted not a second in delivering the finishing strike to each one in turn with his knife.

The battle only lasted a couple minutes, as the final attacking Ravager was thrown by Bren unceremoniously into a heap the hunters had created. Faygo had been seriously injured, and was set at the base of the tree to rest while Konta, Zanzu, and Bren surrounded him for protection. After a few minutes of tense waiting to see if any more descended from the treetop, Konta peeked from underneath the curtain of leaves and signaled for Bobo to do the last part of his job.

The scout unfolded the wings of his Fruit Bat pelt and took to the sky, circling around the tree in great arcs while making the distinct clicks that the airborne predator normally made. Sure enough, his mimicking of the Fruit Bat drove the remaining Ravagers that were hiding high in the Willow's canopy to climb to the ground as they sought shelter from an attack, which made for easy cleaning up by the hunters awaiting them below.

It was only after they had finished piling up the last of the carcasses that they turned to assess the extent of Faygo's injury. It was far worse than they had expected: great chunks of his legs had been taken out by the shredding bites of the Ravagers, and heavy purple blotches were forming under the skin where he had been struck countless times, suggesting bad internal bleeding. His right ear had been ripped off, several teeth were missing, and his left arm was twisted at a terrible angle. With such heavy injuries, it was unlikely he would ever be able to hunt again, even if he managed to heal.

Zanzu motioned for Konta and Bren to go with Bobo and bring the tribe back, while he remained behind with Faygo to tend to his wounds. Konta felt terrible, unable to shake the feeling that he should have protected his friend better. They had been hunting partners since the day they started learning to hunt, and though Faygo often acted unruly and arrogant, he had always been a good hunter and a loyal friend. Still, the security of the tribe had to come above all else, and so Konta hesitantly left the shade of the Weeping Willow to recover his people.

Several hours later, the tribe had packed itself up again and had made the slow, arduously careful journey to where the Weeping Willow stood. Bren had moved ahead and was waiting at the edge of the canopy, signaling that it was still secure and ready to be moved into.

As the tribe began to filter in, Konta rushed to the trunk to see Faygo's condition. Zanzu was standing over the injured warrior with a slight smirk, but before Konta could wonder why, he looked down and was beyond astonished to see that there was no injured warrior there. Faygo was still resting on the ground, but miraculously all of his wounds had disappeared: even his missing ear and the large bites missing from his legs had returned, all in the span of a couple hours. Konta shook his head, completely confused as to how such a feat could be accomplished. When he looked to Zanzu, who had clearly noticed his bewilderment, the massive Head Hunter shook his head and walked past Konta, clapping him on the shoulder in a brotherly manner as he left. The message was clear to Konta: Zanzu knew what had happened, but it wasn't something he had to worry about.

The tribeswomen had already gotten to work securing the tree for encampment throughout Autumn, a task that would put to use that pile of Ravager bodies the hunters had secured. They had already taken a couple of them and slit them open throat to sternum, draining their blood as efficiently as they could into large gourds which they then handed to Tamto. The scout, being well versed in navigating trees, scampered up to the top as naturally as a Ravager might have, and proceeded to empty the gourd of blood all over the leaves, doing his best to coat the entirety of the tree. This imitation of the Ravagers' territory markings would ward off a large number of predators who might have otherwise tried to take refuge in the tree as well. Combined with the thick foliage overhead and the easily covered perimeter naturally created by the drooping leaves, the Willow would make as close to an ideal settling spot as any that could be found to wait out the rains of Autumn.

That night, as the tribe celebrated another quiet Settling around the fire they had built (now safely left out in the open, as the smoke was dispersed as it traveled through the network of branches and leaves overhead), Konta couldn't take his mind off of the impossible healing Faygo had undergone as he watched the newly invigorated hunter showing off some knife-flipping techniques shamelessly for a number of yet to be paired young females. Was it something Zanzu had done, or perhaps some innate power of the Triceraboar pelt that Faygo had that only he knew about?

His mind reeled with questions to the point that he was only awakened from his stupor after a brisk shaking from Kontala, who was wearing such a look of concern that it made Konta ashamed to have been bothered so deeply as to worry her. He decided that the best idea was to shrug off his confusion and be content with his friend being alright and the hunt successfully securing a place for his tribe to get some well-earned rest. The answers, he figured, would come in time.

The Filament Beetle

Getting a day of rest was a rare reward that was not taken lightly by the hunters of Konta's tribe. Constant vigilance was required on everyone's part to ensure the safety of the people, but at the same time, the chief understood the merits of a well-rested and healthy hunter. Earning a day of rest usually involved completing a particularly harrowing hunting expedition, though each hunter eventually, no matter how small their contribution, would be allowed to take time to recuperate.

Konta hadn't been given a day of rest in some time, and so when he awoke the morning after the battle with the Ravagers only to have Murg pull the pelt off his shoulders and place it in his arms – the chief's signal to take a rest from hunting for a day – Konta met it with an inward sigh of relief. As dedicated as Konta was to the protection of the village, even he appreciated the odd day off to be with his mate and take care of small personal matters.

As he washed up in the communal basin, he felt something gently press against his lower back. With a wry grin, he turned to find his dear Kontala, having just risen from sleeping. He swept her into a gentle embrace with arms forged from years of backbreaking labor, reveling in the softness of her wild hair as it brushed against him. She beamed at his youthful excitement, running her fingers through the tangled mess of black that was Konta's hair. The sensation sent a pleasant chill down Konta's spine, and at that moment, he didn't care that he was drawing awkward stares from the other hunters or that the tribeswomen were silently chuckling to themselves. He had been spending a lot of time out on the hunt recently, and other than when they slept, he had barely gotten to be with Kontala. He was going to revel in every second of their time together.

As he stood there in her embrace, he felt a couple faint kicks from her belly. Their child was becoming more active, it seemed, and Konta knew it wouldn't be long before his baby would be born into this world. He mused upon the gender of his child, as he so often found himself doing, while he wandered arm in arm with Kontala over to where breakfast was being prepared. Of course, having a girl would be great for the tribe; the number of girls being born was slowly declining, and at the same time the number of women who could bear children was starting to decrease. Without more tribeswomen being born, there'd be no one to teach the intricate arts handed down solely to the females that allowed the tribe to live as they do, to say nothing of the tribe losing its ability to procreate.

Even so, Konta was hoping to have a young son. It was the one thing he had hoped for, ever since he was a young man being taught the ways of hunting by his own father: to have a boy whom he would teach all his hunting skill to someday, so that he could become a great hunter in his own right and help usher in further prosperity for the tribe.

Konta had been so absorbed in thought that he hadn't even realized he had grabbed some food and was already eating. By the time he snapped out of his stupor, the platter he had been eating off of was already picked clean, and it dawned on him that he had simply been staring off into space, lost in thought for several minutes. He knew full well that being lost in thought was not something that hunters usually did, and the number of people who had been staring at him awkwardly had only increased from the communal basin. Feeling a bit embarrassed, Konta quickly scrubbed his dish clean in the bathing water and returned it, deciding to busy himself lest he waste his precious free time.

Some of the younger ones had been set to the task of keeping the Weeping Willow they camped under coated with the blood of the Ravagers they had stockpiled, a task that would help them build the strength they needed if they ever hoped to survive the seasons to come. Konta watched for a short time as two different groups of young men – both of which seemed to be competing with each other – used two different methods of carrying the blood to the top of the tree where it would be dispersed.

One group each took a gourd and filled them with their cargo, and then climbed as a group up to the top and deposited it on the outside leaves. Meanwhile, the other group was taking an entire Ravager body to the top to disperse its contents. Konta watched in amusement as one fledgling climbed the tree and had his partner hand him the carcass, at which point the second boy would climb to a point higher than the first and take hold of the corpse once up there, allowing the first boy to climb even higher and repeat the process.

Konta was impressed with both methods, as they each strengthened different skills that would become invaluable later in life. The first method was less strenuous but required multiple trips to empty the entire contents of the body, pushing the fledglings to move nimbly and wisely to find the shortest route up and down the tree, whereas the second method took only one trip but required great strength and stamina to constantly hoist the heavy body higher into the canopy, and constant awareness of their surroundings to make sure the branch they were on didn't give out from the weight or the Ravager body didn't get snagged on something.

Feeling a little boisterous at the sight of the competition, Konta walked to the pile of Ravager bodies and slung one over his shoulder effortlessly. For the young men, its weight was fairly considerable, but to Konta such a small creature was so light he hardly even noticed. Then, with the skill borne from a lifetime of training and life-or-death situations, Konta scampered up the trees with as much grace and foresight as the Ravager he was now carrying once had. In seconds, he had passed up both groups and stood at the highest branch, giving a teasing grin to the fledglings below as he waved the Ravager above them as if it were weightless.

As he sat at the top, egging on the groups to strive harder simply with his presence, he noticed the faint odor coming off the dead Ravager in his hand. Even though it was so faint that it was almost imperceptible, it was a scent that Konta was well acquainted with: the stench of death. Already the Ravagers they had saved were beginning to decompose, and before long that precious supply of blood they carried would go just as bad. Autumn had just barely begun, but their greatest safeguard against potential predators would soon be unusable, yet he had no clue as to how the tribe had handled such affairs in the past. Even though Konta knew there were ways to preserve such things, he had only gained his notoriety as a skilled hunter a few seasons ago, and was still learning the inner machinations of how the tribe dealt with these problems. In the back of his mind, he hoped such a plan was in motion now.

After emptying the crimson contents of his carrion over the leaves, only lingering enough to make sure they thoroughly spread across the tree, Konta hustled back down the Willow as easily as he had climbed it, leaving the fledglings in awe of his dexterity. He tossed the emptied Ravager corpse in a different pile that had been erected, where they would be used for food later on. As he walked back towards his tent, thinking to spend time honing his weaponry some, Konta felt a powerful pressure on the back of his neck.

He turned his head, startled, only to realize that it was Zanzu, the Head Hunter of the tribe. Konta had never taken a close look at the behemoth that was Zanzu, but now that he was looking directly into the massive man's eyes, he realized for the first time how startlingly cold and blue they were and how emotionless his expression was, though it was hard to read through the scruffy beard the giant hunter wore.

More intimidating than his stare, though, was the lack of scars on his body. Most every hunter who had a pelt bore some trophy from their past hunts; even Konta bore a few, not the least of which was a massive jagged one that crossed his chest – one that he got from his encounter with the Obsidian Panther. Looking so closely at Zanzu, Konta couldn't make out a single line or blemish that looked like a former battle wound. It seemed unreal that a hunter as distinguished as Zanzu, who had slain a Razorback Mammoth, could not have even one scar visible on himself.

As the two hunters locked gazes for a moment, Zanzu's beard crinkled the slightest bit as if he were smirking, then gave a firm push and began to lead Konta by the scruff. Konta wasn't quite sure what was going on, but there was no way he could struggle against the giant. It was the first time he had experienced Zanzu's strength personally, and the overwhelming power he felt pulsing through the Head Hunter's grip made him momentarily flash back to the Tortoasise. Never before had Konta felt so nervous simply being in the presence of a fellow clansman.

Oddly enough, Konta found himself being led back to his own tent, where he had been going in the first place. Zanzu didn't let go when they got to the entrance, though, and instead continued to push Konta all the way to his bedding. He finally released his hold, and with a firm gesture motioned for Konta to go to sleep. It aggravated Konta to be commanded to rest in the same manner that the children were treated, but he wasn't about to protest against the man who had just proven to him firsthand that, so he chose, he could snap Konta's neck with a flick of his wrist. So Konta complied, and once satisfied, Zanzu left the tent in a hurry.

Konta lay there for a few minutes, mulling over this strange behavior, when Kontala entered carrying a small cup with something steaming in it. He looked over the contents of the cup as she pushed it into his hands, a strange bluish mixture that he had never seen before, but though he was wary to drink something as mysterious as this, one imploring look from his mate was all it took for him to down it in a single swig. It was only mildly warm, which made him worry about why it had been steaming so much, but just moments after finishing the liquid, a powerful sleepiness overtook him. His sight began to blur and his head started to spin, but he could tell that Kontala expected this to happen, as she softly brushed his hair and planted a small kiss on his forehead before leaving the tent.

He knew that there had to be a reason for this odd behavior he had just experienced, but there was little time to wonder what it was as Konta passed into a dreamless sleep.

* * *

The first thing Konta noticed when he woke up again was that he wasn't inside his tent. Someone had managed to drag him out and place him next to the fire pit, where the sudden brightness and heat woke him up, or at least so he assumed. His head still swam from whatever it was that Kontala had him drink, but as if to respond to his addled state, a massive hand appeared beside him holding another cup of something steaming. Konta didn't even have to glance to know who it belonged to.

Seeing Zanzu explained how he ended up outside, but Konta was still curious as to why the Head Hunter had taken such lengths to get Konta rested and active during the night. There was little doubt in Konta's mind that Zanzu was planning a night hunt, but why would he be so keen on taking Konta along when there were several readily capable scouts that could be just as effective?

He decided that it was better to simply make sure he was in his top form for whatever prey they were after tonight and quickly finished the drink he had been handed. Unlike the first one, this one was steaming from genuine heat rather than the chemical properties, and Konta nearly scalded himself by trying to finish it in a single gulp. Still, the strong heat helped get his blood moving and filled him with a new vigor, steadying him for whatever was to come.

Zanzu seemed impatient to get a move on, so Konta hurried to retrieve his weapons for the hunt. To his surprise, Zanzu shook his head when Konta grabbed his usual flint knife and wooden spear, taking them from his grasp and handing him the great hammer made of the strange glinting stone. Most of the time, Konta balked at using the weapon, being so slow and cumbersome, but he knew that whatever it was they were about to hunt must be something that only sheer power could overcome.

The only other things he needed besides his hammer were a few odds and ends for first aid purposes, so it took little time for Konta to be ready to move out. Zanzu took charge, leading Konta to the far end of the Weeping Willow. At this time of night, there was very little activity in the camp, with but a few tribeswomen who preferred to work at this time tending to various tasks like keeping the fire stoked for any scouts returning from their excursions and preparing the things that the other tribeswomen and hunters would use when they soon awoke. Near the edge of the tree's perimeter, a few scouts kept watch from just inside the edges of the Willow's canopy, staring out into the muddled, rain splattered darkness for any signs of danger. They let Zanzu and Konta pass readily, but Konta wasn't quite sure he wanted to go charging ahead into what he saw.

Konta was no stranger to night hunts, even if he wasn't a scout, but a night hunt during Autumn was a completely different experience. It was hard enough to see through the endless downpour when there was still daylight straining through the thick cloud cover; take away that and it became all but impossible to see more than a dozen heads in front of him. Scouts that had nighttime routes during Autumn were the best of the best, somehow finding a way to do their jobs despite such circumstances. Konta couldn't help but feel a bit more appreciative of their efforts as he stood in their situation, where every twitching shadow could be a predator that he would never see coming.

He stuck close behind Zanzu, who appeared to know well enough how to navigate through the foliage. More than once the Head Hunter made sudden turns, and as Konta followed his stride, he was sure he heard some rustling from the direction they had just been going. It was all too well known that there were many types of plants that were just as vicious as any animal, especially during Autumn, and Konta could only be thankful that it was Zanzu he was shadowing now.

Zanzu held up his arm to stop Konta right at the edge of a clearing. Even with so much time to let his eyes adjust, it was still impossible to make out anything other than inky blackness. However, Konta could hear the distinct sound of splashing water, so he assumed that they must be very close to a lake or river. He tried his best to make out what it was, but it proved to be a hopeless attempt. He turned to Zanzu, expectant, but the giant man had grown deathly still and was staring intently in the direction of the clearing. At this point, Konta felt like little more than a bystander, but he was certain that his reason for being here would become apparent before long, so he spent the idle time trying to make out whatever it was that Zanzu was apparently waiting for.

After some time, Konta became aware of a sound that didn't quite match up with the others he had grown accustomed to hearing – a different sort of patter, ever so slightly different from the sound of the rain on the ground or hitting the body of water. The sound seemed to come from somewhere overhead, and it was moving. As Konta looked towards his fellow hunter to see if he had heard it, Zanzu dug into the bag he had brought and unearthed something wrapped in cloth. Without a moment's hesitation, he ripped the cloth off and hurled the object overhand with all his strength.

Konta didn't even have time to wonder what was thrown as suddenly a dazzling light exploded into existence above the clearing. Konta couldn't help but shield his eyes as the brilliant flare illuminated the night sky. When his eyes finally adjusted, he was able to see now that they were indeed at the edge of a clearing that opened to a great lake, the waters frothing from the endless rainfall.

Konta squinted as his eyes shifted to the glowing orb that now hovered some distance over the lake and readily enough recognized the light source as a Filament Beetle, a sort of scavenging insect that had a distinct method of hunting. Rather than capturing prey itself, a Filament Beetle would find creatures that it considered suitable to eat and follow them until nightfall, waiting for the creature to fall asleep. Then, the treacherous insect would fly overhead and explode into the shimmering array that Konta now beheld, instantly alerting every predator in sight to a free meal. In turn, the Filament Beetle was free to help itself to whatever remained of its unlucky victim.

The creature was difficult enough just to find unless it was flashing in its distinct fashion, but it was even harder to capture one. The fact that Zanzu had one on hand was yet another point in favor of his unchallenged hunting skill. Konta, however, was more interested in whatever creature they were trying to flush out with the flare.

It was then that Konta's ears picked up a distinct flapping sound. Something shot across the sky at the bright ball of light, emitting a frantic series of clicking noises, and Konta realized that the Beetle had attracted the attention of an adult Fruit Bat. He hearkened back briefly to a couple of seasons ago, when the other hunters and he had taken out the pups to teach them how to harvest Fruit Bat young, and how he had seen a full-grown Fruit Bat sleeping far ahead. Seeing one awake, however, was a different story. The incredible beating of wings that at full span stretched farther than five adults, the visible contraction of its muscles displaying the incredible strength it needed to keep itself aloft, and the terrible claws and teeth it bared angrily at the unknown disturbance, all of that reminded Konta that this was a creature that could rip him apart before he even had a chance to cry out. Even worse, he knew that it could hunt for many days and nights on end without resting so long as it continued to rain, being able to renew its strength and stamina by absorbing water directly through its body.

Konta tensed, waiting to see how Zanzu would begin the attack on the Fruit Bat. He wondered why his fellow hunter would demand he keep his spear and knife at camp, when those two weapons would have been far more useful against their current quarry than the hammer he now clutched tightly. So tense was he that he didn't even notice the way the surface of the lake began to bubble and churn, and it was only as the surface began to break that he realized that something else had noticed the unusual luminescence of the Filament Beetle.

That something exploded out from the depths of the lake, something long and twisting that careened into the sky and snapped around the Fruit Bat without giving it a chance to react. The Filament Beetle sensed the danger and fluttered higher, but continued to shine, biding time until it could feed. Its brilliance allowed Konta to get a good look at the creature that had caught the Fruit Bat so effortlessly, a gift that Konta wasn't so sure he was grateful for.

What he beheld was unlike any creature he had seen before. It bore a long, segmented neck comprised of over a dozen pieces that gave it the ability to twist and undulate in a sickening fashion. At the end of that neck was a grotesque maw filled with long, translucent teeth that were just barely visible, being they were currently embedded deep in the Fruit Bat's flesh. Its features seemed somewhat reptilian in nature, though its eyes were compounded and more reminiscent of an insect's, but what was truly disturbing to Konta was what he saw within the beast.

Its entire body was somewhat transparent, the light of the Filament Beetle capable of shining well through the length of it, but here and there were dark shadowy forms that seemed to be frozen within the beast. It only took Konta a moment to realize that they were other creatures, likely previous victims of this monstrosity that were still lodged in its throat. Even now, as the creature began to work its jaw and swallow the Fruit Bat it had caught whole, Konta could see the other dark shapes inside this horror beginning so slide further and further down its gullet.

Konta wanted to run. He hadn't the slightest idea what this creature was capable of, but being able to so easily capture and kill a Fruit Bat, to say nothing of the numerous creatures it had already obviously caught, was nothing for two lone hunters to be trying to hunt. He turned to make sure Zanzu was ready to retreat. To his shock, Zanzu was instead stepping out of the clearing and slowly walking towards the edge of the lake. Konta could see that the creature, whatever it was, had already noticed Zanzu's approach. He could only hope that it wouldn't attack with its jaws preoccupied.

Konta's hopes turned to unbridled horror as the waters began to churn again, and another creature identical to the first broke through the surface. Before Konta even had time to believe what he was seeing, a third head also emerged on the opposite side, its teeth gnashing. The two new heads flanked the one that was still feeding on the Fruit Bat, both emitting an ominous fog from their open jaws. Together, the three continued to rise from the depths of the lake, and it was now that Konta could see that all the necks joined at one single, large transparent body.

Zanzu now stood at the shore, and if Konta didn't know better, he would have sworn the Head Hunter was daring the creature to attack from the way he held himself as he looked up at the three monstrous visages that glowered at him.

Without any signal or warning, the two new heads shot towards Zanzu, their long transparent fangs bared and poised to kill.

The Formaldehydra

Time seemed to slow for Konta as he watched the pair of ravenous jaws flash towards his fellow hunter. His mind raced as he tried to think of something, anything he could do to prevent Zanzu from being ripped asunder by the great beast's razor sharp teeth. In the end, all he could do was hope that Zanzu could leap backwards in time to perhaps avoid the worst of the impact.

The Head Hunter did, in fact, make a move, but rather than trying to escape backwards, at the last moment, he sprang forward with a single incredible leap. Konta had never seen a hunter move so quickly in his life, and apparently neither had the great beast, for both heads tried to close inward to catch the spry human. However, they had apparently not expected such a swift reaction, and their sudden attempt to change direction caused the two head to knock together at full force with a cracking sound that rivaled a thunderclap.

The heads of the beast both hit the ground, completely dazed, the only signs that they were still alive being a steady stream of mist that continued to issue lazily from their maws. The third head seemed to realize that its counterparts were in trouble from the way its shimmering eyes turned upon the situation, but it was still preoccupied with the freshly caught Fruit Bat and so was helpless to do anything.

Zanzu was in a prime position to deliver a strike against the creature, as its heads spun around in a dizzied haze from their sudden collision, but instead he turned directly towards Konta and made a motion. For some strange reason, Zanzu wanted Konta to step out from his vantage point and join him on the shore of the lake.

Konta's instincts were still definitively telling him that stepping any closer to this creature was the stupidest thing he could do. It seemed every bit as moronic as walking right up to a Tortoasise or a Razorback Mammoth and openly provoking it. Still, Konta knew that there was no reason for Zanzu to openly expose him to a situation that would do either of them harm, and Konta was curious to see what exactly the great hunter had in store for this horrific beast. So, with one last great swallow and a cold sweat drenching his body more thoroughly than the rain could ever hope to do, Konta emerged from his hiding place, gripping his hammer tightly enough to make his tanned knuckles turn a grisly white.

The monster had recovered its senses before Konta had made it halfway towards his comrade, and its

eyes immediately focused on the arrival of a new target, one that likely looked much less imposing than
the tall and powerfully built Zanzu. Seeing that he
had drawn the creature's attention only made Konta
even warier about the situation, and every cell in his
body screamed for him to turn and run from this
place as fast as he could. It was years of experience
that had given him the ability to assess situations in
a hunt to such a primal degree, and he had no doubt
that it was because he listened to those gut reactions
that he was alive today. It was only because Zanzu
made another impatient motion for him to step out
that Konta was able to force himself to ignore those
feelings and continue towards what he assumed was
certain death.

Without warning, one of the heads reared back
and lunged again, appearing to sense the lack of con-
viction in the new prey's movements. Konta had no
idea how he was expected to fend against this creature, but it was too late to think of flight; he knew he
couldn't hope to pull of the kind of agility Zanzu had
displayed moments earlier. His trusted hammer, the
sturdiest of all his weapons, felt significantly useless
against what was now bearing down on him, but it
was the only thing that he had to defend himself, so
he pulled back with every ounce of strength his could
muster. Adrenaline surged through Konta's veins as
he prepared to attack with what was likely the last
swing he would ever take.

A dark blur shot into the sky, directly above one
of the monster's heads, and landed with a resound-

ing thump. Konta had to blink several times to make sure the rain wasn't causing him to see things, but there was no doubt that the object that had dropped onto the attacking creature was Zanzu. The force of his impact blasted the head into the ground, where it skidded for a distance from its own momentum until it finally came to a rest just within arm's reach of Konta. Up close, the great jaws of this creature were even more intimidating, as there was no doubt that it could swallow Konta whole if he made a venture within its mouth.

However, having the creature so close and in such a helpless position, Konta's instincts kicked in once again, and this time he reacted without hesitation. Hefting the hammer high overhead, Konta brought its full mass down directly onto the open multi-faceted eye of the beast as it spun in its socket in confusion. There was a mighty crunching sound as the strike rang true, and a great spurt of liquid ushered from the wound as the beast let out a terrible screech of pain.

Konta had been analyzing the creature from the moment he first laid eyes on it, as he always did when encountering something he had never come across before, and the more he observed the more uncomfortable he became being so close to it. For one thing, the fog that streamed incessantly from their mouths had a strong, biting odor to it that instantly told Konta it was dangerous to breathe. Being in such close proximity didn't make matters easier, but it did allow him to notice that the body fluid that had been expelled when it was attacked was not blood, or at least not like any blood Konta had ever seen. As he was already well aware, the creature was transparent for the most part, and so he wasn't as shocked as he might have been to see that its blood, too, was transparent, but what concerned him about it was that the acidic odor it gave off, a stench even greater than the beast's breath. Was this monstrosity some sort of giant container of poison?

As if to further cement this theory that he feared, he could see now that the creature's teeth were not like a lizard's teeth, as that was the first thing he compared the beast to. Considering the vast number of creatures he had more experience with, Konta found their appearance more similar to somewhere between a snake's fangs and an insect's stinger – they were hollow, pointed, and slightly transparent like their owners, and it was easy for Konta to see that there was some sort of liquid inside those great fangs. He had little doubt now that whatever this thing was filled with, it was almost definitely something lethal if injected, and that it had plenty of options for dispensing its deadly payload on unsuspecting prey.

The creature flailed in vain to try and escape as it continued to writhe in agony, yet it was unable to wrench itself free with Zanzu still sitting atop it. Konta marveled at how his fellow hunter could pin down such a gigantic creature. Certainly, he was a large man, but to be able to incapacitate such a creature would indicate that he weighed even more than he appeared to, which only raised further questions for Konta.

He was so confounded by the events that were whirling through his head that he had almost forgotten that there was a second head to contend with. As if just noticing the situation at hand itself, the other head opened wide and made another wild lunge at Zanzu, who was still sitting atop his quarry. Without batting an eye, Zanzu leaped off the creature from a sitting position right as its comrade was about to strike, causing the two heads to once again collide painfully. The second head, which had struck with mouth agape, recoiled back and let out a high screech of pain, and Konta noticed that most of its teeth had been broken off and were leaking more of the strange foul liquid that the beast was filled with. It was both a testament to how hard the creature's carapace was, as well as a further indication that its teeth weren't designed to crush or chew as much as they were made to puncture and inject, much like a serpent.

Zanzu had landed some distance off, and Konta saw that he seemed almost placid at the way events were unfolding. It was impossible for him to believe, but there could be no denying that Zanzu was merely toying with this over-sized creature. He had yet to receive so much as a scratch, and even after displaying so many incredible feats of physical prowess, Zanzu .had not even begun breathing heavily.

The Head Hunter locked eyes with Konta and gave a small grin, something that Konta didn't feel comfortable returning in the given situation. Zanzu didn't seem to notice, however, and instead looked back at the creature and gave a sharp whistle. The three-headed beast startled a bit, now clearly wary of the foe they had unsuccessfully attacked twice now. Still, the creature was quite visibly agitated, as the two heads they had been battling swayed back and forth with jaws opening and snapping shut in irritation. Konta mused that the creature had likely never encountered a foe that could so readily thrash it, and was unsure on how to proceed.

Of course, beasts such as those rarely were able to adapt to new situations quickly, and sure enough the creature shot forward again to try a third time to get Zanzu. The head that Konta and Zanzu had injured remained behind, as did the one that was still feverishly trying to swallow the Fruit Bat, so it was only the one head that had broken some of its teeth off earlier that now approached at blinding speed.

Zanzu smirked at the attack and held out both his hands. The events that happened next flew by at a pace Konta could barely keep up with: The head collided with Zanzu, who caught its jaws with his bare hands and held them open as his heels dug into the ground. The creature's strength was great, but it only managed to force Zanzu a short distance back before it was unable to overcome him any further. The moment the creature had been stopped, Zanzu twisted the head sharply, causing its neck to snap and a spurt of clear liquid to erupt from the cracks in its carapace. The head went motionless, save for the slight twitching of its jaws, and the other two heads screeched in unison, though whether it was because the heads could feel each other's pain or because of blind rage, Konta couldn't tell.

The great beast began to retreat into the water, but before the head could slide too far away, Zanzu ran to where the neck had cracked and pulled from his back the bundle he had brought from the village. Without waiting to unwrap it he stabbed the instrument directly into the wound, driving it straight through the creature's neck.

Zanzu turned and shouted incoherently at Konta. Normally something like that would cause Konta to panic, but at this point the creature they were fighting had made so much noise that it was unlikely that any more would make much of a difference. Zanzu had already proven how reliable he was in such situations, so Konta felt more comfortable than he would have thought possible running up to his fellow hunter. Zanzu eyed Konta's hammer, which Konta had been holding idly since the last attack, and then looked pointedly at the edge of what he had forced through the creature's neck. Konta understood what Zanzu wanted, though he had no idea what it would accomplish.

Konta raised the hammer and struck the piston with all his force. There was another great cracking sound, and Konta had to turn his head away as another spurt of clear liquid shot from the wound. When he turned back, he saw that the force of his blow had caused the head to sever cleanly from the neck, and though the headless tube continued to slither back into the depths of the lake along with its brethren, the chitinous skull remained behind, its jaw still opening and closing from sheer reflex.

The remaining two heads had already disappeared beneath the lake's surface, which was continuing to froth as the great form sunk deeper into the waters. The lifeless neck that had just been relieved of its head was the last part of the beast to vanish as it was dragged into the depths, all the while leaving a trail of pungent body fluid behind. After just a few moments, only the lingering smell of the creature's blood remained as a reminder of the ordeal Zanzu and Konta had just undergone.

Zanzu had wasted no time in procuring a large tarp that he had brought with him, and quickly wrapped the severed head within it, tying the ends together and handing the bundle to Konta. Despite the un- nerving trial he had just undergone, Konta didn't hesitate to take the load and secure it to his back. It was lighter than he had expected given its size, but it was still a great burden, and sloshed as if it were filled with water, making it difficult to balance. Once Konta was sure he had a good handle on it, he nod- ded to Zanzu, who took charge and started leading the way back to the camp.

As the two broke back into the foliage they had come from, Konta noticed that the shimmering light that had illuminated the lake had yet to fade behind them. He looked up to see that the Filament Bee- tle had begun to follow them. Undoubtedly it had noticed the distinct lack of food left behind for its efforts, and so had started following them in hopes of drawing predators towards the hunters so that it could feed.

Zanzu had noticed this as well, for the moment the Beetle became visible through a break in the canopy overhead, the great hunter crouched down and shot into the air at an impossible speed. Before the Beetle could react in the slightest, Zanzu had snatched it in his hand and wrapped a cloth around it, where the insect's light still continued to stream through feebly for a few seconds before finally extinguishing itself. The Head Hunter landed on a tree near Konta, quickly hopping from branch to branch until he was again at ground level, making not a sound during his descent.

Though the Head Hunter made light of his incredible feat, urging Konta to follow him with haste back to the village, Konta was feverishly trying to figure out what Zanzu *was*. There was no possible way that Zanzu could be pulling off the feats he had displayed tonight unaided. It was far beyond the scope of even the greatest hunters Konta had witnessed in his life. Still, he couldn't imagine any kind of pelt that could bestow the kind of reflexes and displays of strength that Zanzu had performed when facing down that terrible three-headed beast or catching the Filament Beetle again. The only reasonable conclusion to Konta was that Zanzu was something beyond a mere human, but what that was, he couldn't figure out.

What he did know, though, was that he was undoubtedly brought along almost solely to bear witness to Zanzu's ability. His contribution to the hunt was minimal at best, and Konta knew that anything he helped with, Zanzu could have done by himself just as easily. The biggest question on Konta's mind was, why did Zanzu go through such lengths just to demonstrate these things to him?

Konta was surprised to find the trip back to the village was much shorter than he recalled the trip to the lake being. Perhaps it was because of all his musing on the subject of Zanzu, but that only further worried him; it meant he had completely drifted off into his mind on the way back, a trait that would get a hunter killed in most situations. He could only assume it was because he had felt safe to do so, because of the safety that Zanzu afforded him. Still, it was not a state of mind he felt comfortable indulging in. Becoming dependent on the skills of another would only cause him to slack off in his own development.

Zanzu led the way past the scouts who were still standing guard, several of whom turned and looked curiously at the great bundle that Konta had strapped to his back. The Head Hunter paid no attention to their gawking, though, and steered Konta towards one of the larger tents that had been erected in the camp, which was used as a sort of medical facility. Inside the tent, the two hunters were met by Murg and a cadre of tribeswomen who appeared to have been waiting for the duo to arrive. Without a moment's hesitation, the women swarmed around Konta and bustled the cargo he had been carrying to the table, where they eagerly unwrapped it. The horrific maw of the strange armored creature was still grimacing at the observers, though its eyes were clearly glazed with death.

Once they were assured of what they had been brought, the tribeswomen split up and began procuring several different odds and ends, though for what Konta was still unsure. Several went into the corner of the tent, bringing out a massive basin that looked much like the large communal basin the hunters used to bathe in; meanwhile, others had grabbed several containers that had been set nearby and were brimming full with water, which they began to pour into the basin. A small number had gone to the storage pouches where various tools were kept to prepare medicine with or to perform surgeries, returning with a number of stone tools, and the rest had taken to lifting the head and placing it in the basin, which was now roughly half full with water.

The tribeswomen wasted no time in using the tools they acquired to begin perforating the dismembered beast head with numerous holes, causing copious amounts of its terrible smelling body fluid to escape confinement and mingle with the water. Konta hadn't realized it before, but Zanzu had bundled the head in just such a way so that the open neck of the beast faced upwards while Konta carried it, preventing this fluid from spilling to the ground, confirming Konta's suspicion that it was this strange clear fluid that had been the true goal of their hunt.

The blood (or whatever it was, for Konta was still indecisive on that matter) caused the water to turn to a murky yellowish color, and he took notice at that moment that the women were all wearing gloves while handling the beast's head, in addition to face masks they had donned while preparing the items for whatever it was they were doing now. It caused Konta a bit of unease that he had breathed so much of that creature's foul breath and the horrid stench of its fluids, but there was little use in worrying about it now.

Zanzu tapped him on the shoulder, signaling for Konta to follow once more. Konta wasn't sure whether he had the fortitude to go on another excursion tonight, but thankfully Zanzu only ended up leading him to the pile of Ravager bodies near the trunk of the Willow. The Head Hunter hoisted a large armful of them and began back towards the tent, so it only made sense for Konta to do the same, though he was only able to bring a fraction of what Zanzu had walked off with.

Konta walked through the flaps of the tent just in time to see Zanzu drop the entire armful of dead Ravagers directly into the basin, which was now full to the brim with the yellowed fluid mixture, causing some of the sickly concoction to slosh over the sides. Konta brought his share over and repeated the process, careful not to get any of the mixture on him. He watched as the long-deceased bodies slowly sank into the fluid, and suddenly Konta remembered what he had just been thinking about the other morning.

Could this be the answer to the question he had in the back of his mind this whole time? Was the blood of this beast some sort of preservative that would allow them to keep the Ravagers from decaying? He knew that when certain foods were preserved by the tribe, sometimes a strong-smelling liquid was used in the process. It would make sense that these creatures would be preserved in a similar manner.

The two hunters took only a couple of extra trips to deposit the entire collection of Ravager specimens into the basin, which the tribeswomen quickly sealed off with a great lid. Konta and Zanzu helped move the basin back into the corner, where it would keep the corpses safe until they needed to be used at a later time.

Zanzu clapped a great hand on Konta's shoulder when everything was finally finished, his beard crinkling in that way it always did when Konta thought he was smiling. Taking that as a sign that the job was well and done, he gave a small nod and returned the smile and left without a single glance back. He had experienced quite enough tonight and was quite looking forward to the sanctity of his own tent.

It only took Konta a few moments to toss his hammer and provisions next to his other belongings, lay his Obsidian Panther pelt carefully over everything, and collapse on the soft Danderdeer bed on the ground next to Kontala, who still had some time before she awoke. Though he thought he had been careful to not wake her, he was surprised to feel her roll over and wrap her arms around him, pulling him as close as she could with her belly protruding as it was. He wanted to turn and return the embrace, but suddenly realized the extent of his exhaustion, and so could only return the gesture by gently squeezing her hand.

As he drifted off into sleep, his thoughts were on his beloved beside him and their child, but he knew that in his dreams, his mind would be focused on the dread beast he had discovered that night: the terrible Formaldehydra, whose name was just as new as the experience Konta had facing it down with Zanzu. Though Konta knew the encounter was yet another stepping stone in becoming a great hunter, he also knew that the encounter would haunt him for many nights to come. Unfortunately, it was a situation he was well used to and gave up indifferently to the nightmares that awaited him.

The Fog of Rafflesion

After the encounter with the Formaldehydra, the weeks of Autumn that followed seemed rather dull in comparison to Konta. Peace was something often sought after and rarely found by the tribe, so it was fortuitous that day after day passed with no real threat bearing down on them as they camped underneath the Weeping Willow. With the Ravagers properly preserved, they had no shortage of blood to continue coating the tree with, and the lack of predators attacking the encampment indicated that their efforts were not going to waste. The hunters had managed to secure several great catches on their expeditions, not the least of which was an adult Fruit Bat that would make excellent rations for the grueling Winter that lay just around the corner. Zanzu had even managed to secure an incredible find in a mature Kogyu Cow, whose meat was nutritious enough to last the tribe for a year if conserved properly.

Still, Konta's hunt for the Formaldehydra with Zanzu had changed something inside of him. He began to realize just how little he really knew about the world around him, and seeing Zanzu's incredible feats against the great beast made him understand how far away he was from being a top hunter in the tribe. Konta was frustrated at his ignorance, but so long as the tribe was at peace, he knew there was little reason to fret over such petty problems. There were more important things for him to worry about than his hubris at the moment.

For one thing, Kontala was nearing the time of childbirth. She had swollen so greatly now that she could not do anything other than the most menial of tasks and had to rest constantly while even performing those. The other women of the tribe seemed to bustle harder with each passing day to carry Kontala's burden, for they knew better than any man in the tribe the strain that came with having a child.

Konta spent what little free time he had available tending to her every need, all the while imagining the type of life he would have once he had a pup to look over. It was a more exciting and terrifying idea than any hunt could be, but what he worried about most was Kontala having to give birth during Winter, when the weather would be at its harshest and the dangers would be greater than any other season.

Even when out on hunts, he found his thoughts constantly drifting back towards his mate and their future progeny. After a close encounter during one hunt where Konta almost fell prey to a Puffer Hippo, a fiercely territorial creature that was so resilient the tribe had yet to hunt one successfully, Murg had apparently noticed how distracted he was and placed him on a rest period. Konta felt thoroughly ashamed of himself, though as he mused over the predicament, he wondered if other hunters ever felt these kinds of emotions when they were expecting a child.

It was only a few days' hiatus before Konta was sent back on the hunt again. Autumn was entering its final days, and every hunter was working extra hard to make sure that the tribe had enough supplies to make it through Winter. Once the seasons shifted, there would be almost no food to hunt or materials to procure for kindling and medicine. Konta was teamed with Faygo, charged by the eldest tribeswoman Marg to lead a group of four less experienced hunters on a search for some useful plants. Both hunters were equally ignorant when it came to first aid matters – that was the territory of the tribeswomen – but Marg thankfully provided some small samples of what she wanted so they could easily compare and identify what they needed. A scout had already found a location where several specimens were growing, so the hunting group only had to be pointed in its direction, and they were off.

Konta was thankful to have been assigned a task with Faygo, whom he felt a closer kinship with than any other hunter in the tribe aside from his Kontala. They were roughly the same age and had learned the tools of the trade right alongside each other. Both were distinguished hunters on their own, but together they created a considerable force in the tribe. Konta was right alongside Faygo when he felled the Triceraboar that the latter now wore as his distinguishing hunter's pelt. Even though Konta didn't directly help kill the beast, for a hunter could only wear a pelt if he killed the creature by himself, Faygo insisted that night that Konta shared in his victory supper, made from the meat of the Triceraboar that he had killed. Normally, no hunter would ever share such spoils with another, so the fact that Faygo was so adamant about it made Konta realize how important his presence had been to his friend. Konta had made it a point to return the favor when he returned from a hunt with the Obsidian Panther in tow, further cementing the bond he felt with his childhood partner.

He had almost gotten lost in thoughts of the past when a swift blow struck him around the head. Konta startled and turned, only to see Faygo giving him a sly grin and shaking his head slightly. It was embarrassing for Konta to be scolded by Faygo, but he also knew that his friend had only the best in mind for him. He needed to focus on the hunt and stop letting his mind wander aimlessly, or he might suffer a fate similar to the one he escaped just days before. On top of that, he was supposed to be teaching the younger hunters how to deal with Autumn's conditions.

So Konta spent the next few hours silently coaching the fledglings alongside Faygo, teaching them how to keep themselves from leaving footprints in the abundance of mud, conditioning them to listen for noises above the constant din of the rain, and showing them how to effectively erase their presence in an instant in the case of an emergency. The last one Konta and Faygo had a bit of fun with, playing a sort of improvised game of hide-and-seek with each other where one would hide, and the other would lead the young hunters in trying to find them.

As their training session continued, they stopped periodically to collect the plants they found along the way that matched the samples Marg had given them. Faygo turned this into a bit of sport with Konta as well, as they both tried to collect as much as they could carry quicker than the other. While Konta had always been better with a spear, Faygo's dexterity with his knife was some of the best in the tribe. Faygo could draw his blade from where he strapped it to his ankle, pare away the plants cleanly, and sheath the knife again before Konta could pull his own from his waist. The contest was practically over before it started, though Konta still made a good showing.

Before long there were only a couple plants left to find, and it seemed Faygo's playful mood had taken control of him. He suddenly lunged swiftly and silently through the foliage ahead of the group. Konta couldn't help but smile at the sudden enthusiasm of his partner and instructed the young hunters to wait for a moment so Faygo could get a head start. One last hunting exercise would be good for their development.

After just a few short moments, Konta started leading the fledglings into the thicket he had seen Faygo disappear into. His friend was an expert of camouflage to the point that he could have made it as a scout, so Konta knew he'd have to be on his toes if he was to have any chance of finding Faygo. He was keen on keeping an eye open for any sign that would tell where Faygo had been – a broken twig, a misplaced leaf, a scruff of moss would do.

Dampening Konta's chances even further was a slight mist that had started to noticeably creep through the overgrowth. Trying to find something hiding in the brush was difficult enough, but compounded with limited range of visibility, Konta realized that there was almost no hope of tracking his partner. It would be hard to find him at best, but the fog itself was a dangerous foe to be tempting; there were plenty of creatures that took full advantage of what the mist brought with it, and Konta certainly didn't want to deal with one when his only support was a gaggle of half-trained whelps. He knew Faygo would return fairly quickly once he saw the fog, so the best course was to just wait where they stood.

At least, that's what Konta had planned to do. As the fog continued to drift lazily through the foliage, something skittered on the outskirts of his vision. He tensed immediately, crouching into the surrounding brush and silently urging the fledglings to do the same. He wasn't sure if they had been spotted yet, but he couldn't chance waiting around for Faygo any longer. He'd had to retreat at the first possible opening.

Again, something caught his attention, a blur of movement from behind some nearby trees. He strained to try and see what it was, but it had disappeared as quickly as it came. Was it hunting some other prey and failed to notice the group, or was it simply biding its time and waiting for them to drop their guard for a moment?

A third flash of movement came, and now Konta realized that whatever was darting about, it was no Autumn beast, or at least not one he had ever seen. The upright body, the long strides, the glimpse of hair and exposed flesh: it had to be human, whatever was moving about.

Konta realized that it could have been Faygo, trying to regroup with the others. Konta stood and made a small motion towards the trees, hoping to grab his fellow hunter's attention without making noise. The shape stirred but seemed to have wandered further off. Taking a chance, Konta made a strange series of clicking sounds with his tongue – it was the most noise hunters were willing to make in hostile territory, which was to say just about anywhere. Still, the figure didn't seem to creep any closer.

Konta was not cocksure or stupid enough to think that he knew all the dangers that lay in waiting in the world, so even though he had never seen a beast that closely resembled a fellow human, he was quite open to the possibility of one existing. At the same time, he wasn't about to let Faygo continue to wander around in the fog by himself, looking for their group. He turned to the fledglings, still huddled on the ground, and signaled for them to wait for his return. He could only hope that today's practice in stealth would be enough to keep them safe as he ventured into the overgrowth after the mysterious shape.

It was slow going for Konta, now that he knew that something unknown was lurking nearby. He had to get close enough to confirm what it was before he could take any other action, but if he moved too quickly, he would give away his position, and at this point, he wasn't willing to commit wholly to the idea that what he was chasing was indeed Faygo. So, he was forced to creep, bit by bit, covering his tracks as he went. Whoever – or whatever – he was chasing appeared to have the same idea, for Konta was unable to find any signs of a trail from his quarry.

The creature had finally stopped moving, giving Konta time to close the distance. The fog had thickened even further, making visibility so low that he had to get within a short stone's throw of it before he could make out any distinguishing features. To make things more difficult, the trees overhead seemed to have grown so intertwined that they blocked out the rain in this area, so the patter of the rain no longer concealed any errant noises he might have made, and a slightly sweet smell filled the air. Konta had to make sure to approach from downwind, lest his stronger odor immediately give his presence away. Still, he was glad to see that whatever he had been tracking seemed frozen in place as he inched forward, careful not to let so much as a single leaf rustle.

He was just starting to make out some details on the shape when it turned sharply in his direction. Konta froze, his hand flashing to where his knife lay strapped at his side. He was prepared to strike out at the thing and run the moment it tried to strike him.

What he wasn't prepared for was the sight of Kontala stepping towards him, her hair falling gently around her shoulders and a hand resting gently on her enlarged belly. It was an impossible sight: the tribeswomen never left the village without a hunter's escort. Even more so, no woman would think of wandering around while carrying child, especially if they were as far along as Kontala was.

Yet there she stood, her dark brown eyes staring straight into Konta's. Their gazes were locked for what felt like minutes, while Konta's mind filled with questions. Then without warning, she turned and began to run off deeper into the trees.

All at once, Konta forgot all bearing of where he was or the dangers that might have lurked. He charged ahead through the plants, running with all his might to keep up with her. The pace that she was setting boggled his mind; how could she run so fast with the child she bore? Even going his absolute fastest, he was barely able to keep up, let alone catch her. Nothing about this seemed right, but for some reason he felt himself continue to chase her deeper into the forest.

In the back of his mind, he started noticing some disturbing things. For one, despite the thinning number of trees, he could no longer see any sign of the rain. He knew full well that the endless downpour of Autumn was just that – endless. There was never a break in the rain until the coming of Winter, and that wasn't for some time yet. Also, the fog had been growing thick to the point that Konta could barely see his hand held out straight in front of himself. Somehow, despite this, he could make out Kontala some distance away, and only by following her directly did Konta avoid running into a fair number of trees.

Nothing made any sense, and yet still he was compelled to continue chasing. The sweet smell from earlier flared powerfully into his nostrils, sending his mind reeling as he tried his best to figure out the situation. Kontala vanished from sight without warning, and Konta impulsively charged forward in the hopes of catching a glimpse of her again. So, it was little surprise that, running so fast with barely a wisp of visibility, Konta collided head on with something.

The force of the impact sent him reeling backwards with his breath knocked out of him. As he fell to the ground, he struck his head, not so hard as to hurt him badly, yet still enough to make his vision swim a little. As Konta tried to shake off the dull ache, his eyes began to focus more clearly on what he had run into. Slowly, two long stalks glazed into view, protruding from a great bulbous shape. The pain in Konta's head began to subside, but as it did, the shape shifted out of view.

Realization struck Konta like a thunderbolt. This was no ordinary mist; it was a cunning trap, and one that Konta had just blundered right into.

Without hesitation, he whipped the knife from his side and brought it across his forearm. Not a deep cut, but enough to hurt immensely. Without pausing, he grabbed a handful of dirt and rubbed it on the wound; this had the double effect of clotting the gash so it wouldn't bleed as much, and also causing the pain to flare sharply.

The fog seemed to lift before his eyes until only a faint hint of it remained. The rain started pelting him relentlessly the moment he tore at his skin, and the sweet smell that had been overloading him before faded to almost nothing.

Konta had seen pictures of the Fog of Rafflesion before in the scrolls he had to study as a young hunter. Since getting field experience against some creatures and plant life was too dangerous, only hand-drawn accounts of these things were available to prime new hunters on their dangers. Even looking back, Konta could remember the image of a hunter enthralled in a shroud of white mist, forced into the clutches of a flower larger than a man. He knew that there were creatures and plants in the wild that could beguile the eyes of a hunter, making them see things that weren't really there. They were considered amongst the most dangerous of all, for they attacked the mind directly with little defense available. The only thing known to counteract this effect was a great deal of pain, effectively shocking the person out of their strange visions.

Now Konta beheld one of these creatures for himself. The massive plant stood in front of him, with fat red petals protruding from the top of its giant jar-like stem, and a slow but steady stream of pleasant smelling mist dribbling from the large opening in its top. It almost mirrored the picture he had seen of it, save for something that was jutting oddly out of the top: a pair of legs. Konta turned a ghastly pale as he noticed the flint knife strapped to one of them.

Without pausing to think about it, Konta grabbed Faygo's motionless legs and heaved as hard as he could, trying to wrench his friend from the clutches of the plant. They came away more easily than the heft of a body should have allowed for. They came away without a body attached.

Konta had to fight back a wave of nausea at the sight of it. He hardly needed to look within the plant: such carnivorous ones were not rare by any means, and he knew perfectly well of this kind, which were hollow and filled with all sorts of strange chemicals that could dissolve through living creatures in a frighteningly short time. When coupled with the mind-altering effects of the Fog of Rafflesion's namesake, however, it became something much deadlier and far more horrifying than any of its peers.

It dawned on Konta with a sickening pang that if Faygo's legs hadn't been sticking out, he would've run headlong into the gaping pitcher plant, and the situation would be Faygo pulling him piece by piece out of its acidic maw. Even in death, his friend had helped him immeasurably.

Konta knew that there was nothing more he could do. Faygo had undoubtedly been snared by the plant's lure and drawn towards it, falling in while still under its spell. The only thing Konta could hope as he trudged back towards the fledglings was that Faygo's death was not a painful one. Though he feared he had lost his bearings, he was able to quickly retrace his steps, for in his maddened dash, he had left a blazing trail in his wake. He moved as quickly as he dared parallel to it, fully knowing that now there was a far more real danger of something coming across his path.

Nothing had befallen the pups, much to his great relief. They looked around at Konta's arrival, expecting Faygo to pop up any moment and scare them. Konta walked slowly past them, signaling to follow. They hesitated for a moment before realization dawned on their faces and they slowly fell in behind Konta, grief visible on their faces.

The rest of the day Konta's mind was in a blur. They had procured most of what Marg had asked for, and in plentiful amount too, but he didn't remember giving their harvest to her. When Murg approached Konta's group and noticed the absence of Faygo, the elder chief shook his head solemnly and eyed Konta with what was undoubtedly disappointment and reproach. Konta barely even noticed. A small part of him in the back of his mind wondered if he'd ever be assigned to a hunt again, after everything that had

befallen him, but for the most part, his mind was oc-
cupied with a hundred booming questions.

Why had he seen what he did when he was caught
in the Fog's control? How did it make him see Kontala so vividly, as if she were truly there? What part
of his brain did the creature contort and poison to
so utterly enrapture him that he couldn't even notice
the world around him? What had Faygo seen in the
moments before his demise?

In the end, he knew none of these things mattered. As he lay down on the floor of his tent, Kontala
leaned close and touched him gently, but even the
comforting touch of his mate barely registered with
him. The man who had grown up beside him and supported him without hesitation was gone forever, and
unlike the stinging gash on his arm, this wasn't a pain
that would go away any time soon.

The Zero Celberus

The endless rain stopped.

It was as dreary a midday as it ever was during Autumn, and Konta's tribe had been going about their daily routine with the normal care and concern they had always shown. They knew that Winter was just about to encroach on them and had already begun the preparations for their inevitable migration to a new campsite when that change came. Tents and equipment were packed, food stored, and all signs of their settlement hidden or destroyed to mask the presence they had made over the span of the season. Konta, who hadn't been sent on a hunt in the last couple days, had secured all of his and Kontala's belongings and placed them in a corner of their tent. It was one of the last ones to remain standing for Kontala's comfort as she drew ever closer to giving birth.

Konta was going to the communal fire pit to heat some water for her when he noticed that the soft white noise of the raindrops against the Weeping

Willow was absent. He stood motionless for a moment, straining his hearing to make sure he wasn't mistaking things, but after a few tense seconds he bolted to the base of the tree and began to climb. Some of the hunters and tribeswomen bustling about looked at him curiously, but others had also begun to look around with an air of unease, undoubtedly noticing what Konta was trying to confirm.

He reached the top with little time wasted and cautiously poked his head from the top of the canopy. The dark grey clouds still hovered angrily overhead, but Konta couldn't see or feel a single raindrop as he peered around. A sharp wind picked up, sending a chill down Konta's spine as it stung his face.

There was no time to waste: Winter wasn't just on its way, it was here. Konta practically tumbled down through the branches in his rush to get back to the camp, only narrowly avoiding hurting himself as he landed on the hard-packed earth. He had just started making his way towards the chief's tent, only to find himself face to face with Murg, who had been waiting patiently for him at the bottom. The chief gave him a quizzical look, to which Konta responded with a single nod. It was all the confirmation Murg needed, and without another second to spare, he trudged off, motioning for everyone to collect their things immediately. If Winter had already begun, then the tribe was in big trouble if they didn't head out immediately.

Konta scrambled to his tent, rousing Kontala from her nap. She glared at him angrily for a moment, but one look at his face told her that there were more pressing matters to attend to. She slowly pulled herself to her feet with Konta's aid and set out of the tent while Konta deftly disassembled their mobile shelter, attaching whatever he could to his back and bundling the rest under his arms. Normally, the younger men of the tribe would heft the equipment while the hunters defended the tribe as they moved, but time was of the essence at this point. As if to emphasize their plight, another frigid blast of air coursed through the leaves of the Willow, almost knocking Konta off balance as he struggled to regroup with his people.

The rest of the tribe were following suit, not being strangers to sudden departures. There was a huge crowd of villagers already waiting near one end of the tree where Murg stood side by side with Zanzu, both patiently waiting for the scout that had been sent out to return with the other scouts and hunters that were abroad. It took little time for everyone to be accounted for by the two, but the impatience could clearly be seen on their faces. Every moment they weren't on the move was another moment less they had to reach a safe place to camp for Winter.

Knowing that the worst was yet to come, Konta had taken precautions and already wrapped himself snugly in as many wraps and cloaks as he could, topping them with his Obsidian Panther pelt. Hunters were not normally allowed to wear their pelts when they were in resting periods, and even though he had only been off the hunt for a few days, getting to don his prized pelt once again was like being greeted by an old friend that he sorely missed. Once he was se-cured, he took the remaining coats he owned and adorned Kontala with them. She almost had to push him away as he tried to force a sixth layer of clothing on her, but Konta's worry for how Kontala and their child would fare in the freezing temperatures won out, and she reluctantly struggled into one last cloak.

With a single wave, Murg urged on the tribe into the bitter cold. The heavy cloud cover overhead still refused to release so much as a single drop of mois-ture, but the tribe members knew all too well that soon they would unleash a flurry of snow and ice, and that, when that happened, they had best be un-der some cover. The rest of the tribe had already fol-lowed Konta's example, bundling themselves in half a dozen cloaks apiece while still making sure they had enough freedom of movement to get away in case something attacked during the migration.

The wind was blowing fiercer and colder than ever before, and the dense foliage that had sprung up dur-ing Autumn seemed to tell their time was near, as several had already shed their leaves, while others had been completely uprooted as if giving in to the fierce storm front that was drawing inevitably closer.

The tribe never wandered without direction. Though their campsites often varied slightly each seasonal rotation, they had developed an intricate knowledge of the lay of the land and knew of sev-eral areas that had suitable spots to set up their makeshift village. It was one of these places that they were heading towards now: a large cliff similar to their preferred Summer camping spot, with a massive fissure that provided enough space for the tribe to camp, while also sheltering them from the harsh elements and creating choke points that aided in defending against any predators.

The cliff had just begun to crest into view when Konta heard a soft but sharp gasp cry out beside him. He turned just in time to catch Kontala, who had begun to crumple to the ground with a grimace on her face. With a great whoosh, a large amount of water poured out beneath her, and instantly, Konta was shoved aside by most of the tribeswomen as they began to bustle worriedly around his mate. It only took a moment for him to realize what was happening, and he could feel the color drain from his face and a terrible knot twist in his stomach. His child was on its way, and it couldn't have picked a worse time to try and come into this world.

Murg saw the commotion, and though he kept a strong expression on his face, there was a slight furrowing in his brow that any seasoned hunter could tell was a sign of intense agitation on his grizzled face. He tapped Senga on the chest, motioning towards where Kontala lay. The young hunter nodded, and walked over to assist – Kontala would have to be carried until the tribe found a suitable place to settle.

Konta had already unfurled his tent, refashioning it with the poles into a slapdash stretcher, which he set on the ground next to his mate. Gingerly, he and Senga lifted Kontala and placed her on the tent hide before they each took the tent pole ends and hoisted her above the ground. The tribeswomen who had jumped to her aid were busy clawing through their pouches for various medicines and ointments, which they took turns coaxing her to ingest or adorn as the tribe started again towards the cliff face.

It was painfully slow going. Worse, the hormones and fluids Kontala was giving off in her current state attracted the unwanted attention of predators. The hunters were forced to fight off an attack from a Boal-lista – a large snake capable of firing itself from the trees like a high speed projectile – and then almost immediately afterwards from a small pack of Rav-agers that had likely been migrating from whatever Weeping Willow they had been nesting in during Au-tumn. At one point, a Filament Beetle appeared and hovered overhead, shining brilliantly as it tried to draw attention towards the tribe. Konta watched as Zanzu, just like he had seen before, lunged into the trees and sprung into the air at an incredible speed. The Head Hunter caught the insect in a thick wrap before plunging back to the ground and landing with-out the slightest injury and pocketing the creature.

The tribe managed to make it to the edge of the giant rock without suffering any great damage, but Konta knew that it would take another day of travel before the tribe could reach the hollow in the cliff face where they camped before. Under other circum-stances they could camp near the cliff's edge for the night and make for the fissure in the morning, but Kontala's birthing complicated things far worse. A woman having a child in the tribe had to be handled with incredible delicacy, and that meant that Kontala and her baby could not be moved for several months' time. She would start giving birth before morning came, which meant that they would be unable to move the village until the tribeswomen, who oversaw the birthing and weaning process of the infant, gave it the okay. They would have to set up camp where they were for the season.

The women wasted no time in erecting a large tent and ushering Konta and Senga to place Kontala inside it. No sooner had they placed her on the ground than the two hunters were shoved outside without another glance. Senga hurried off to help set up the rest of the village, but Konta stood in front of the tent with a jumble of emotions floating inside of him.

He knew the procedures for a new life being born: the woman would give birth in the tent, and both she and the baby would stay in there under constant supervision of most of the other tribeswomen. He had no idea why this was done, only that it was a necessity and that it was a great danger to the whole tribe to disturb the process in any way. Every precaution would have to be taken to protect the tent until his Kontala was permitted to leave by the other tribeswomen.

Grima, the mother of the small girl who Konta helped save last Summer, stepped out from the tent and began pouring a pungent, translucent fluid that Konta recognized as Formaldehydra blood around the tent. The tribe usually used Desert Squunck musk as a deterrent to predators, but they had used the last of it up earlier in the year. Fortunately, the strong scent of Formaldehydra blood would be a passable substitute, and the tribe had taken plenty with them when they left their last encampment.

Konta felt a tap on his shoulder and turned to find Zanzu handing him a large gourd full of liquid. Popping the top off and taking a slight sniff told him it was another container of Formaldehydra blood, and Zanzu motioned for him to follow. Konta assumed they were to set up an odor barrier around the outskirts of the village, judging from the similarly full gourd Zanzu still held under his arm.

For such a barrier to be effective, it had to encompass the village in such a way that their tents would not be visible from the edge of the ring, which normally was aided by the help of rocky outcroppings or vegetation surrounding their camp. With the precarious location of their current campsite, however, the ring would have to be much wider, to discourage predators long before they got within range of the camp.

Zanzu and Konta walked along the edge of the mountain they had camped next to until they could no longer see any sign of their camp and began the slow process of creating their invisible barrier. Konta took the first shift, carefully emptying his container and making sure to not pour an excessive amount of the foul liquid as he strode out in his best estimation of a circle around the village. He got a good distance out before his gourd was empty, at which point Zanzu took up the task, employing the same care that Konta had been taking.

By the time both their flasks had been emptied, the light had begun to fade from the sky, and fat snowflakes had already begun to descend from the sky. Though the winds had lightened slightly, there was still a biting chill in the air, and Konta knew that it would grow far worse once the Sun had completely set. Even though they had only covered about half the distance needed to completely encircle the camp, the two hunters had met up with Bren and Grim, who had been performing the same work from the other side of the village. Their combined efforts had effectively covered all the ground they needed, and so the four hunters prepared to return to the camp and set themselves up for the night.

It was as Konta began to turn to head towards the camp that Bren caught his shoulder and forcefully turned him towards the open plains that lay in the other direction. Something was moving out there, an erratic movement that was undeniably some creature wandering around, making its way unsteadily towards their location.

The snow had been falling long enough to pile up a fair amount, and the hunters all crouched and buried themselves in it the best they could. It was almost unbearably cold and uncomfortable, but it was also the only effective way to hide when no cover was available. Konta watched closely as the unknown beast crept closer, sometimes staggering off a slightly different direction, but never straying from moving in their general direction.

Even in the dimming light, Konta was finally able to make out the shape as it lumbered ever closer. Its four limbs padded unevenly but incessantly as the beast dragged itself along, its sheer white fur making it difficult to see through the snow flurry that continued to fall. Three large lupine heads lolled at its forefront, blackened tongues drooping lazily from all of its maws, which were hanging open to reveal three sets of razor sharp fangs. Konta fidgeted uncomfortably, realizing that their camp was being approached by a Zero Celberus.

This particular beast was a pure native of Winter, much like Snow Gremlins or the Razorback Mammoth. While other beasts were sometimes found by the tribe in various states during multiple seasons, including Fruit Bats or Kogyu Cows, native creatures only appeared during their respective seasons, and they were assumed to migrate to other climates that better suited them as the years occurred. The Zero Celberus was just such a creature and one of the many reasons that Winter was so dangerous for the tribe. Only the hardiest of beasts had adapted to living in the relentless freezing temperatures, and these beasts wouldn't hesitate in the slightest to rip the village apart in their never-ending quest for food, scarce as it was in the tundra of Winter.

There was something off about the Celberus that now approached, however. Its movement was erratic, as it several times stumbled and narrowly avoided

falling over altogether. Even though its path was undeniably heading towards the camp, there was little
method to its movement, as it strayed several times
off to the side before returning to its regular path.
Undoubtedly it had picked up the scent they had left
behind in their trek, especially with Kontala in tow,
but such a beast would in that case move with care
and intent purpose, not the strange staggering gait it
now showed. What's more, each head was letting out
a soft whimper or growl, something that no predator
on the hunt would ever do if they intended to hide
their presence. As Konta took careful observation of
the Celberus, he noticed that there was a white film
around its three mouths that was unnoticeable until
now, seeing as how it blended with the creature's fur.
This Zero Celberus was terribly sick, and even worse,
it could communicate this disease with a single bite. If
it managed to get to the village, even in its weakened
state, it could potentially injure an untold number of
tribesmen and women. At this point, it wasn't clear
if it would be deterred by the barrier, but Konta knew
they couldn't take the risk that it would breach.

Attacking a Zero Celberus under normal circumstances was risky enough; their strange physiology
had adapted so that their heads held no brain. Instead, all their vital organs were cushioned well
within the depths of their body, likely to help them
keep warm in the brutally low temperatures. Because
of this feature, the three heads were like complex
limbs, though they still functioned as the eyes, ears,
nose, and mouth for the central body. Cutting off

one head had about as much effect as cutting off a human's hand, so the only effective way the tribe knew to incapacitate one was to sever all three heads. Though this wouldn't kill the creature, it would effectively remove its ability to see, hear, or smell its foe, at which point they could attempt to strike its vitals; the vicious tenacity of the Celberus would make it almost suicidal to try and fatally wound it while even one head still remained.

Compounding the standard danger of the beast was its illness, which made receiving even a small injury from it a fatal proposition. The four hunters would have to coordinate perfectly to strike it quickly and decisively, taking off its heads before it had a chance to fight back.

The hunters looked at one another, trying to figure out an order of attack that would be most productive. Grim tapped himself on the head, touching the edge of his pelt made from a sea creature Konta knew as the Cnidanglia, a gelatinous bell-shaped creature. Its dried body was so translucent that it was almost invisible as it sat on Grim's shoulders, but Konta also knew that what lay concealed beneath the cowl was their best bet for stopping the beast long enough to allow the others to strike.

With a simple nod of acknowledgment from the other three, Grim waited until the creature had wandered almost uncomfortably close to their position. They had hidden themselves close to where their odorous barrier had been set up, and by good fortune, the Celberus stopped at the edge of the ring and visibly staggered as its delicate noses were assaulted by the overpowering smell. Without waiting to see if it would continue on or not, Grim erupted from his hiding place. As he did, a countless number of long, thin strings trailed off from the folds of his pelt: the tentacles of the Cnidanglia. The Celberus let out a snarl of surprise as Grim laced the fine threads all around the beast, entangling it effectively. It tried to turn and snap, but the hindrance of the dozens of roping tentacles slowed it down enough to give Konta and Bren time to lunge and spear two of the heads to the ground before it could react to the arrival of new enemies.

As the creature tried to get its bearings in its disease-addled state, Grim quickly regrouped his strings and securely tied the muzzle of the last head closed. The creature struggled against its captors, who had to fight with every last ounce of their power to keep the Celberus pinned down, even as sick as it was. Fortunately, they didn't have to hold it for long. Zanzu emerged from hiding with his spear in one hand, and in the other a great heavy blade hewn from solid obsidian, its edge known well amongst the tribe for how wickedly sharp it was.

As always, Zanzu's efficiency was unparalleled. He drove his spear through the head Grim had tied down so the latter could free his pelt up before the Head Hunter cleaved the great obsidian blade through all three heads in a single swing. Liberated from the body, they slid down the spits they were still affixed to, eyes rolling around madly in the last throes of death. The body, however, was still very much alive, and with nothing pinning it down it began to lunge around wildly. Without a single head, the creature was unable to keep track of where it was or guide itself in any capacity. Konta was curious how it hadn't bled to death with such serious wound. For that matter, there was barely a drop of blood staining the ground.

Though the creature continued to thrash, Grim had left one of his pelt strings attached to the ankle of the beast. With a single deft tug, he pulled its leg out from underneath it, causing the headless Celberus to topple to the ground. It seemed to try and right itself, and then appeared to finally understand the futility of its situation and simply lay still, undoubtedly exhausted from illness and exertion. Konta approached it with his fellow hunters cautiously, noticing that the stumps where its heads once were had iced over, preventing the wounds from bleeding. He knew that such things could happen in such cold climates, but also knew that blood froze much slower than water did; something about the Zero Celberus' blood caused it to freeze unnaturally quickly, a trait that Konta found most confusing in a creature that lived only in cold climates.

With Grim using his pelt to once again securely tie up the creature, despite its lack of resistance, Bren proceeded to listen closely to the creature's torso, evidently looking for where its vital organs were kept. Though Zanzu was the greatest amongst the hunters overall, Bren had been a hunter for over twice as long as Zanzu and was more versed in the anatomy of beasts than any other. It only took a short time for him to come to rest on one spot, pausing there for just a moment before nodding in affirmation. He took his Everlasting Redwood spear and drove it through this singular spot. At once the creature convulsed in pain, unable to let out a cry of anguish, but this suffering only lasted briefly as it fell limp, without so much as a twitch.

It was a complete victory over the creature, but as the four hunters turned to head back to camp, there was a decidedly bittersweet tang to it that Konta at the least felt. It was certainly necessary to kill the beast before it had a chance to come in contact with the villagers, but there was no use for the meat of a creature that was so far gone with disease. Its pelt was equally useless for the same reasons, a terrible shame considering the cold the tribe would be suffering through for the next several months. They had fought and killed a terribly dangerous beast but without any of the rewards that naturally came with it. All they could do was leave the corpse there, hoping that perhaps other creatures would be wary of coming so close to something that reeked of disease, and thus steer further clear of the village.

The return to the village was unceremonious, with the villagers all bustling about to try and make decent living accommodations for the unbearable freezing temperatures they were to experience later that night. Zanzu slunk to the chief's tent, likely to inform him of the kill they made so Murg could warn the scouts to steer clear. Bren retired to his own tent, as he needed more rest than the average hunter at his age; on the other hand, the youthful Grim had already begun helping other tribesmen erect their tents.

Konta knew he could go to sleep now if he wanted, and he was fully ready to do so, mentally and physically exhausted as he was from a day of rushing around. Unfortunately, his tent was still inside the tepee where his wife had been taken when she went into labor. There was no chance that they would move Kontala to get the tent out underneath her, and Konta knew that he wouldn't want the tent now anyways – it would be far too pungent and attract predators. More likely than not, it would be destroyed when the birthing process was done.

Still, he found himself standing just outside the birthing tent, watching intently. The tribeswomen who were in there helping Kontala give birth wouldn't be coming out any time soon, and Konta wouldn't be able to get any information from them until they were done, to say nothing of going in to visit his wife and newborn.

Had the child been born yet? What did he or she look like? How was Kontala's condition? Konta knew that women sometimes died in childbirth, a thought that sent his stomach reeling. For the next several months, he would be in the complete dark, though there was cold comfort in knowing that as long as the child was alive, that tent would stay up until they were done.

Two sharp taps on his shoulder drove him from his thoughts, turning his head to see that Grim was now beside him. Grim was a man who had only lived through a couple of years more than Konta, but his experience spoke volumes more than that. Like Konta, he had yet to receive a bracelet acknowledging the chief's favor, which was something that baffled the former; of all the hunters aside from Zanzu, Grim usually returned with the best catches when he went on hunts, and with the fewest injuries.

Konta watched as Grim stood there, eyeing him oddly for a few moments. The latter ran his hand through his short brown hair, kept clean and even with a flint knife. In comparison, Konta's hair ran wild and tangled, completely unkempt, though he hardly cared considering it was usually hidden under his Obsidian Panther cowl. The gesture Grim was making made him look oddly young, Konta found that somewhat funny, considering how old he felt at that moment.

After a strange interlude of the two standing and doing nothing, Grim put an arm around Konta in what seemed to be almost a comforting gesture. Konta allowed himself to be led by the hunter to another tent, which he assumed was Grim's. Sure enough, stepping through the flap brought him face to face with Grimzi, the girl Konta had helped cure of Desert Flower poisoning during Summer. She greeted Konta with a hug that could have been mistaken for a tackle, almost completely taking him off-guard. Grimzi's face beamed and she almost laughed, only stopping when Grim shot her a reprimanding look.

It was now that Konta noticed that most of his things had already been placed inside Grim's tent. He worried how cramped the tepee might end up becoming when Grima was also taken into account, but then Konta remembered that Grima was one of the tribeswomen tending to Kontala. With an insistent gesture from Grim, Konta reluctantly lay himself down on the bedroll set out for him.

If he hadn't been so weary, he would've worried about the perils of the months to come, exposed as the tribe was with no chance to relocate. He would've worried about the health of Kontala and his child, hoping that they would be able to survive the hardships of Winter. He would've mused on the unexpected kindness of Grim, a hunter whom he rarely spent time with, perhaps seeing this kindness as a form of repayment for helping Grimzi. There were a hundred things he would've thought on, but instead he slept a deep sleep, devoid of dreams and nightmares. Those would come soon enough with day's break.

The Blight Mare

Winter was a time of radical changes for the tribe, in terms of the way they functioned from day to day. It wasn't enough to take the normal precautionary measures and hope that it was enough. For the beasts that thrived in the unforgiving wrath of Winter's cold, the tribe would be like a bountiful harvest if they were caught unaware. Guard duty had to be tripled, sleep was kept to the barest of minimums, and hardly any hunting parties were sent to scavenge for food. These measures were even more crucial now that their safety had been compromised from being forced to camp in a sub-par location, with Kontala's unexpected labor.

If any blessings could be counted amongst the list of hardships facing the tribe, they had already secured a sizable surplus of food over the past year, especially during the Autumn that had just gone. With stores of preserved Fruit Bat and jerked Kogyu Cow already set aside, there was no shortage of provisions to help them weather through the tough weeks that were to come.

For Konta, Wintertime also marked a larger change in his daily routine. Of course, this time of year brought with it continuous snowstorms, blanketing the ground and making everything almost blindingly white. This was an obvious disadvantage for him, who wore the pelt of the Obsidian Panther – a creature with jet black fur. Trying to hunt during the day would make Konta stick out against the landscape dangerously, all but announcing his presence to any predator in sight. Sure, he could technically hunt without the pelt on, but besides losing the benefits of the Obsidian Panther pelt – the extra claws as a backup weapon and the tough fur for protection – a hunter who abandoned wearing his pelt was seen as being incapable of adapting to situations and looked down upon for it. Even if it was mostly social dogma, it was so deeply ingrained in Konta's behavior from his life of growing up with the tribe that he would rather radically change his hunting strategy than be without his coat. So, during Winter, Konta changed his role in the tribe to a scout, using the cover of darkness to more effectively hide himself in the wild on the rare occasions that he had to leave the village.

Despite suddenly changing his role amongst his people, at this point there would be little reason for him to leave the village. He would be needed to help keep watch and there was no need to hunt for food with the stores they had, which meant mostly his change in routine involved sleeping through the day and guarding through the night. With Kontala still cloistered within the birthing tent, Konta didn't have anyone to tend to as he had these last several seasons, so his days and nights passed by uneventfully as he awoke when the clouds in the sky began to darken more and didn't retire until well after light began to try and stream through the overcast sky.

So, it was with a bit of a shock one day that Konta, trying to sleep as best he could, felt a small nudge at his foot. Normally, a tribesman who was trying to rouse him from sleep would do so with two sharp taps on the shoulder, so the unfamiliar sensation made him bolt awake immediately and reach for the hunting knife he kept close just in case. He shot upright with weapon poised to see a long snout poking curiously at his feet. The creature lifted his head, letting out a soft snort in surprise at the sudden movement. It eyed Konta warily with large, watery eyes, and now Konta could more clearly see its shimmering white short haired coat and realized that he had been roused by a Blight Mare.

Konta's heart skipped a beat, and he hastened out of his bedding and into several layers of clothing as quickly as he could. He tossed his pelt on his head before leaving the warmth of the tent to better assess the situation. Sure enough, the first thing that greeted his sight as he slipped carefully past the beast at the mouth of his shelter were several more Blight Mares shuffling about the campsite, walking from tent to tent at a leisurely pace.

Blight Mares were one of the few species Konta knew of that didn't eat living creatures. In that way, they were considerably less dangerous than most other beasts when encountered abroad. There was no threat of being attacked by them unless they were provoked; Blight Mares were scavengers by nature. However, this fact was cold comfort when coupled with the fact that the creatures were also extremely voracious in their eating habits – herds of Blight Mares were usually very large and needed a lot of food to support their numbers. Their highly sensitive sense of smell allowed them to find potential food sources from miles away, and once they got the scent of a meal there was little that could stop them.

It was no surprise, then, that they would be able to smell the tribe's provisions and find the camp. This wasn't an uncommon occurrence for the tribe, but it was also normally more easily managed when the tribe was firmly tucked within its usual mountain crevice and able to drive away a herd before it could try to squeeze into their village. Exposed in the open as they were, though, there was no way to stop the Blight Mares from simply trotting in and ravaging their campsite. The strong odor of the Formaldehydra blood they had placed down wouldn't be able to mask their presence to the Blight Mare's nose. Konta inwardly cursed at their lack of Desert Squunck musk, which would've been far more effective than the blood if they hadn't already wasted the last of it during Spring.

Other hunters had already met in the center of the village, where a large fire sat burning under the tribe's Sponge Whale tarp. Two hunters stood outside the covering with sticks, making sure to constantly knock the snow that fell incessantly on the tarp so that it didn't melt and eventually drip onto the fire. The others stood or squatted around the open flame, some of them staring sternly into the fire while others looked out with dark expressions at the numerous animals lolling around the village. Konta could relate to their feelings, as this situation was one that was both dire and difficult to solve.

Whether or not the Blight Mares would attack them at the moment wasn't the concern, but rather the question of how to evacuate them from the campsite. The Blight Mares wouldn't leave on their own account until they had consumed everything in the area that they found edible, which of course would be all the provisions the tribe had collected for the season – even with their stores buried in the snow as they were, it wouldn't take the invaders long to sniff out their caches. Trying to chase the beasts off with force was a dangerous gamble; the Blight Mares might strike back if threatened, and they were known to kick with enough strength to crack stone. Even worse, they would most certainly begin to cry out to warn their herd, which would give away their position to any nearby predators instantly. To top things off, even if the herd did leave, their ensuing stampede would trample everything underfoot without mercy.

157

Still, the tribe couldn't leave things as they were, or they'd be picked clean of food and would have to resort to hunting during Winter, a prospect that would put the hunters in great danger and would run the risk of not being able to forage enough food for the tribe to make it through the season. There was almost no chance of getting rid of the Blight Mares without running one of the risks they had already considered, but there was no time to consider what would be the best course of action- something had to be done now.

Konta was tired and exasperated from both lack of sleep and the weight of the worries on his shoulder regarding his mate and child. With the stress of the task in front of them, he could feel himself nearing a breaking point. More than anything, though, he was sick of the helplessness he felt from the days and nights of simply staying hunkered down in the village, waiting for a threat to strike his people. At that moment, he decided that he had stood around passively long enough: if nobody else had an idea, he'd take it into his own hands.

Near the edge of the awning stood Zanzu, his brow furrowed in thought as he likely mused over the same things Konta had just been thinking. Konta approached him and gave him a couple of taps on the shoulder, drawing the giant man's attention. With only a few curt gestures, Konta motioned to the tribesmen around them and then towards the wall of the cliff, near the birthing tent where Kontala lay. Zanzu looked him in the eye for a moment, and though the Head Hunter would normally never take

such rough commands from another hunter, something in Konta's visage must have convinced him. He
quickly grabbed the attention of the other hunters
underneath the tarp and motioned for them to group
up where Konta had suggested. Meanwhile, Konta
had already started to rush around the campsite,
pointing every tribesman and tribeswoman he could
find towards the same area. Zanzu took the hint and
followed suit, and in short order, the two had managed to corral the whole tribe into the area. Murg was
the last to arrive, a look of confusion on his face as
to what was about to happen.

While Konta had been scrambling around the
camp, he had also been on the lookout for something
crucial to his plan. It didn't take long to find, but he
had to make sure that everyone was in place before
he could move things into action; things were about
to get very chaotic.

Once he was sure everyone had been accounted
for, as confirmed by Zanzu, Konta rushed a short
distance off towards a specific Blight Mare he had
found. This one was clearly distinct from the others,
as it was crossed with scars and sported a long, thick
mane down its head and across its back. It stood a
good head taller than the rest and was visibly much
more muscular: a Blight Mare stallion.

Oftentimes during past Winters, it had been
Konta's job to do reconnaissance hunts in order to
gain an experience and knowledge in a time before he
had earned his pelt. One of these vital jobs had been
to chase off herds of Blight Mares if they strayed un-

comfortably close to their settlements. The one thing that stuck out more than anything in Konta's mind from those hunts was the formation that the herd took when on the move: one lone, powerful creature leading sometimes over a hundred of its kind in a great stampede that threatened anything in its path. For all the Blight Mares that Konta had seen, never did he see more than one stallion in any given herd, and he had witnessed firsthand that this one stallion was the pivotal member of their societies. It wasn't difficult for Konta to understand why: when almost all of the herd was a single gender, the only way to continue propagating was to protect and rally behind the few instances of the opposite sex that were available.

Now that lynchpin to the survival of the Blight Mares' herd ambled just ahead of Konta, its nose intently sniffing for anything it could eat in the camp. The animals obviously had little contact with humans, to be so fearless with so many of them in the immediate area. It was an advantage that Konta knew he would only be able to exploit once, and he wasn't about to waste that chance.

Konta approached as cautiously as he could, not wanting to frighten the creature or provoke it into lashing out at him. He was within arm's reach of the beast when suddenly Konta lunged into the air and landed sprawling onto the stallion's back.

Instantly the Blight Mare stallion reacted, rearing onto its hind legs and neighing loudly. The heads of dozens of Blight Mares rose and turned in the direction of the sound, now aware that something had threatened their otherwise peaceful grazing. Konta, meanwhile, was struggling to keep his grip on the beast, knowing that the moment he was cast from its back, he would be trampled mercilessly beneath its hooves. Instead, he clutched and pulled desperately at its mane, further enraging the beast as it began to buck back and forth in an attempt to rid itself of its attacker.

Somehow Konta managed to cling on long enough to tire the creature to the point that it had to stop struggling for a moment. It was all the moment Konta needed to swing himself upright onto its back. Now straddling the beast, he pulled his feet back and kicked his toes into the stallion's underside. Normally such an awkward kick shouldn't have meant much to such a brawny creature, but before he had jumped the stallion, Konta had slipped the leggings of his pelt onto his feet, complete with the finger length claws that protruded from its pads. As the dagger-like instruments dug into the Blight Mare stallion's flesh, it let out a braying cry of pain and, realizing the danger it was in, took off at a blinding speed in an attempt to both throw off Konta and put as much distance between itself and the threat of the humans as possible.

In this precarious position, Konta didn't dare loosen his grip for a moment to look behind him, but in the end, it wasn't necessary. Even with the thick snow blanketing the ground, he could hear the sound of hundreds of hooves as they began to pound the ground together in unison. The Blight Mares were following their stud's lead, even if it meant leaving such a plentiful food supply behind. Likely they were trampling tents underneath as they moved, but Konta could at least breathe a sigh of relief knowing that all the tribesmen were safe against the wall of the cliff. Now he had just one problem to deal with: how to escape with his own life.

Being scavengers as they were, Blight Mares could never go head to head with the terrible carnivores that hunted during Winter, so the only other option when encountering these creatures was to run, and they were amply capable of this. Their long, powerful legs propelled them through the snow banks, kicking up a huge cloud of frost as they thundered onward. Konta knew that if he were to try and jump off now, he'd undoubtedly be trampled by the innumerable Blight Mares following close behind their stallion leader, but he also knew he couldn't hold on for much longer, and every moment he remained on the horse he was being pulled further and further from his village with only the flint knife strapped to his side and the claws on his pelt to protect himself on the trek back.

There was a sudden burst of snow to Konta's right, followed by a bellowing roar. The Blight Mare stallion startled and made a wild and sudden turn that Konta wasn't ready for. He toppled off, thankfully cushioned by the snow as he rolled a short distance and finally came to a stop. He instinctively winced, preparing for the pounding hooves to pummel him to death, but after a few seconds passed without event, he braved a glance around and saw the herd swerving sharply, still following their leader's charge without so much as a glance at him.

It was then that Konta also saw what had erupted so unexpectedly from the snow: a Polaroar, a giant bear that, like many other predators, claimed Winter as its hunting grounds. The massive carnivore was hot on the heels of the charging Blight Mares. One of the horses turned too quickly as it tried desperately to escape and slipped, falling on its side. The Polaroar was on it instantly with razor sharp teeth and claws, its immense strength crushing its prey's bones with every swipe of its powerful forelegs. The Blight Mare barely had time to cry out in terror before it was silenced, flesh being ripped from bone as the great bear wasted no time in beginning its feast.

Konta had already pulled his Obsidian Panther pelt from his shoulders and flipped it inside out, stowing it safely inside his wraps in a desperate attempt to make himself as invisible as possible. He had to make his next move slowly and carefully, for drawing the attention of this predator would be the end; he'd have no chance of outrunning a Polaroar, and the weapons he had on him were woefully inadequate for defending himself against such a monster.

As Konta slowly crawled away on his belly, doing his best to ignore the biting cold and avoid cutting himself on the claws of his pelt that were pressed uncomfortably close to him, a terrible sound rang through the air: a high-pitched howl that seemed to continue lingering long after it had stopped. It was the sound of a White Wolf.

If the Razorback Mammoth was considered the king of Winter, then the White Wolf was surely the prince. It was a creature of ferocious grace and cunning, hunting in tightly knit packs that together rivaled all but the most brutally efficient predators. Few beasts would try to take on a White Wolf, as there was no such thing as finding one on its own. For any one Wolf seen, there was sure to be a group somewhere nearby, waiting to strike.

Though the howl had been a distance off, there was every chance that the Wolf in question had been calling to its comrades near Konta's location. The Polaroar hadn't missed the call either, its head turning sharply as it looked for any impending danger. Nothing had crept into sight yet, but no creature was stupid enough to wait around to see whether or not a pack was on its tail. With a grunt of irritation, the Polaroar stood and loped away, leaving its hard-earned meal to likely be stolen by the White Wolf pack. In the end, it was better to sacrifice a meal in hopes that it would distract a predator than to try and take the prey along and weigh itself down.

Konta held his breath and threw himself as close to the ground as he could as his eyes darted around, looking for any sign of movement that would give the Wolf pack away. Sure enough, after just a few moments there came another piercing howl, this one much closer than before. Konta looked towards the sound to see the majestic form standing near the crest of a snowy hill. As the Wolf began to make its way down towards the Blight Mare carcass, Konta noticed that it wasn't as majestic as he initially thought. Its steps were strange and uneven, and its legs moved completely unnaturally, almost as if the beast was dangling on something...

Now realization and relief crashed onto Konta, and he ventured raising his head and giving a short whistle. The White Wolf's head turned, the legs once again swinging strangely at the sudden move, and now there was no mistaken the dark color just underneath the Wolf's jowls: a human face. It was no true White Wolf, but rather Bren donning his pelt of the beast.

At the signal, Bren stood tentatively and started towards the sound in a low crouching position, ready to drop down at the first sign of a potential threat. Konta still didn't dare stand, since his wraps, though light in color, still stood out much more than Bren's solid white pelt. Instead he crawled on his belly, doing his best to cover himself in snow as he went along. It was slow going, but considering that neither had planned on being out in the open right now, it was the best plan of action to avoid pulling attention to themselves, especially when, by now, predators might be picking up the scent of the freshly killed Blight Mare lying out in the open.

Once the two met up, Bren started leading the way back towards camp, Konta being grateful to have a guide considering he had no idea how far he was from the village or what direction it was in. The pace was literally a maddening crawl for the most part, and darkness had already begun to encroach on the two before they crossed the Formaldehydra blood barrier that marked the outskirts of the village and felt safe enough to finish the journey on foot.

While they made their way back, Konta wearily dusted the remaining snow from his shoulders and put his Obsidian Panther pelt back on, trying his best to fight the terrible chill running through his body. Some of the snow that had been piled on him had melted simply from his body heat and had soaked through his wraps. The cold bit at him without re-morse, and he was thankful when he could finally pick up his pace to try and get his blood flowing.

To his surprise, Bren struck him around the head with an open hand as he put his cowl back on. It was the type of firm blow Konta often saw parents give their children when they did something danger-ous and stupid, but the weariness and cold he had been fighting through all day made it hard to figure out what warranted such a rebuke. As if reading his mind, Bren jabbed at his pelt, then Konta's, then pan-tomimed as if he were a predator about to strike, end-ing his act by making a motion with his fingers like something with four legs running.

As tired as he was, even he could figure out what Bren was trying to convey. If he had given his idea to run the Blight Mares off a bit more thought, he would've realized that, rather than riding the stallion out of the camp, he could have simply scared it off by doing what Bren had done with the Polaroar: use his pelt to make it run off. It would've likely had the same effect, without putting Konta in danger in the process. In hindsight, Konta realized how foolish and unnecessarily perilous his plan had been.

And yet, even though Bren's expression was stern, he put his hand on Konta's head and gave him a reassuring pat. Regardless of how stupid the plan ended up being, in the end Konta had chased off the threat, and nobody had been hurt, so there was little reason to be completely angry at him.

At least, that's what Konta thought until they finally made it back to camp, at which point it seemed every adult in the village took their turn of approaching him and striking him on the head just as Bren had done. He got the message fairly clearly: he wasn't to ever pull such an idiotic stunt again. When everyone had had their turn at rebuking him, though, nobody could hide the smiles plastered across their faces. Things could have gone much worse, and all things considered they had gotten off with hardly a scratch; the tepees and tents that had been knocked over in the stampede had already been erected again, and save for some hoof marks, there was no permanent damage to anything.

Konta immediately went to sleep at the first possible moment, having lost most of his usual sleeping time from the day's excursion. When he woke up later that night, ready for his shift at guard duty, he was surprised to find a veritable feast waiting for him at the mouth of Grim's tent, steam pouring off of it in defiance of the cold outside. It was far more than was usually rationed to hunters during Winter, since food had to be stringently conserved. Just the sight of it made Konta chuckle silently: between this gesture and the scolding, the knowledge that he was so valued by the tribe warmed him more than anything else.

The Snow Gremlin

There had never been a Winter that tested Konta's constitution more than this one. Every night that passed without incident only further stressed his nerves as he waited for the inevitable strike of a predator to shatter the peace, and every day was full of fitful sleep as he woke constantly at any small sound, fearful for any attack.

The fact that nobody had left Kontala's birthing tent in weeks was a mixed blessing. No news was good news, but being kept in suspense during an already difficult time did no favors to Konta's state of mind. Sometimes, as he sat around idly on guard duty, he would watch the entrance with rapt attention, hoping to see any sign of his mate and their new child. The most he ever got was a quick glimpse of the tent flap opening, only to have one of the midwives either taking in food that was set out for them, or else placing out the used dishes to be collected. This would usually dishearten Konta, leaving him to turn sullenly back to his watch, but it was never long before his attention was drawn once more to where the fate of his family lay.

It was in this manner that most of Winter ran on, as Konta kept watch over the encampment with most of his fellow hunters through the dark and freezing nights. On rare occasions, he would be sent out to scout in close proximity to the camp, if only to see if any predators were on the approach, but nothing had ever come of these ventures, and so he would return to watch and wait once more.

One particular night, the stoic hunter was greeted by a great snow flurry as he stepped out from Grim's tent to prepare for another shift of guard duty. Stormy weather wasn't always a given during Winter, as there were plenty of days where not a single snowflake would fall, but when they did come it meant higher tension for everyone keeping watch. While the blizzards did help conceal their poorly hidden village, the danger of beasts that could be hiding just out of sight in the flurries far outweighed that one small convenience. Unlike during Autumn, where the same problem persisted, they were nowhere near as sheltered as they had been under the Weeping Willow, and the creatures that prowled in Winter were of a different caliber of threat.

The communal fire in the center of the village was being tended by a couple of the younger hunters, who were doing their best to keep it stoked with dry wood and clear the snow from the tarp overhead.

Konta was grateful to see the large stone bowl that had been set over the top, filled with steaming water ready for use in cooking or bathing. He scooped up a handful, the heat blissful on his freezing hands, and rubbed it vigorously on his face to wash and wake up. He blinked the water out of his eyes, feeling the last vestiges of weariness slip away as he dried himself thoroughly next to the fire; walking out into a snowstorm while wet would be a foolish thing to do.

He reached down for his spear, ready for yet another long night watch, when there came a yelping noise from a short distance away. Konta froze in shock for but a moment before bolting towards the sound, recognizing it as one of the tribesmen in pain.

One of the young nameless hunters lay on the ground, blood slowly seeping from numerous wounds dotting his arms and legs and staining the snow-covered ground with splotches of red that stood out clearly even in the darkness. Several of the tribesmen and women who had been within earshot were already trying to help the injured boy, who Konta could see was beginning to shudder. Looking closer, Konta noticed that the boy's wounds were small punctures in his skin and alone would likely not be terribly dangerous. On the other hand, these tiny holes had been punched all over his exposed limbs. It appeared that the boy had just woken and had yet to cover himself for the weather.

Before Konta could begin to process what to do next, there came another cry from elsewhere in the encampment. The villagers tending to the boy before them looked at each other in worry, but with a swift motion, Konta signaled for them to stay put, and with that he took off to investigate the new disturbance.

This time it was a tribeswoman who lay on the cold ground with her vital fluids blotting the area around her, whom Konta recognized as Bobo's mate, Bobono. He leaned in close to examine the wounds, and sure enough, she bore the same markings as the young hunter he had just left behind. Her injuries were much lesser, only dotting the exposed portions of her face, neck, and arms as she had already wrapped up thickly to go about her duties. Still, Konta could tell the source of these wounds at a glance, and the recurring attack in such a short time only confirmed his fears.

Now the villagers who had been asleep began to emerge from their tents with anxious looks on their faces; the sound of a human crying out for any reason was more than enough to rouse even the soundest sleeper in the tribe. The sight of one of their own lying prone and stained with blood was enough to send those who hadn't already brought weapons with them scurrying to the tents to arm themselves.

There was a flash of movement off in Konta's peripheral, and he turned sharply to see a small creature standing a short distance from him. Its body was oddly shaped, with bumps and bulges rising from its being with no apparent reason, and it was covered in fur the color of the snow that still whirled through the encampment. It stood teetering on two hind legs, with stubby forearms that stuck out of its sides as if it were trying to hold something up. Most disconcerting was its face, or rather its lack thereof, for there were no discernible eyes or mouth anywhere on the beast, though it emitted a series of high pitched chitters from somewhere on its body. Its appearance confirmed Konta's worst fears: the tribe was under attack by Snow Gremlins.

Snow Gremlins were not a beast to be trifled with lightly. They only attacked during storms such as the one they were currently suffering and could effortlessly vanish and hide in the howling flurries, waiting for an opportune time to strike. What was worse was that the tribe's conventional weapons were woefully inadequate for dealing with the Gremlins, as they would disappear into the storm before a hunter could get close enough to deliver a blow. There was much that the tribe didn't know about the Snow Gremlins, but there were two things they were certain of: they always attacked in large numbers and only fire could definitively drive them away.

Without waiting for the predator to make the first move, Konta dashed towards the communal fire to arm himself. The tribe would have to light as many torches as possible and set them around the camp, a task that would require a lot of coordination. Fortunately, Zanzu was already waiting at the fire with several branches, their tips doused in strong-burning oil from the Tulamp flower. The Head Hunter had placed several more in the fire and began handing them silently to the other hunters who had caught wind of the threat and knew what had to be done.

Before Konta could reach forward and take some torches for himself, another cry rang out not far from their location. He turned on reflex to see Senga lying on the ground and bleeding, a torch still burning next to him where he had dropped it. Konta took a few steps forward to try and help him, but at that moment a powerful gust kicked up and obscured Konta's vision. Though he only lost sight for a moment, he saw as the wind died down that a Snow Gremlin had crossed his path in that short interval. His grip tightened on the knife he had been holding, but knowing the weapon would be useless, he forced himself to turn on his fellow hunter for a moment so he could snag a torch from the flames that still licked at the full basin. He turned and threw the torch at the beast, but it simply hit the ground with a dull thud. The Gremlin was already nowhere to be found.

Several more shouts of pain floated out in the distance, and the hunters who had been gathering around the fire split up with torches in hand to tend to the situations as best they could. Konta hurried to Senga's side, but thankfully the young hunter's wounds were few and easy to cover using the wrappings he already was wearing. Once he was sure Senga was safe next to the fire with Zanzu, Konta took hold of the two torches that still lay flickering in the snow and took off immediately for the one place he knew to be most vulnerable to attack: the birthing tent.

The camp was in a frenzy, with people running every direction as they tried desperately to fend for themselves and their fellow tribesmen from the enemy that seemed to be able to ambush them from thin air. Several torches had already been set up around some of the tents, but he had to make sure that those in the birthing tent were secure before he took any other action at this point.

Another gust shook past Konta when he suddenly felt two sharp, painful pricks on his shoulder where his cloak had slipped a bit in his hurry. He looked down, but snow had already covered where he felt the pain. He brushed the snow off so that he could get a better look at the wound, but the moment he did an intense pain shot through his arm starting at the shoulder. He bit his lip to keep from crying out and now could plainly see the large puncture in his skin, where blood was already beginning to run down his arm. Konta had no time to waste tending to himself, so he simply tightened his cloak as best he could and forged himself forward.

As he rounded a corner and the tent came into view, Konta was struck with a wave of dizziness. His eyes slid out of focus, and it took all his willpower to keep himself from toppling over on the spot. Was there some sort of poison in the creature's bite? This was the first time he had ever been injured by a Snow Gremlin, and he recalled no recordings of poison from the medical tomes they kept on hand to catalog the dangerous properties of the various creatures. Of course, few tribesmen who had been attacked by Snow Gremlins had survived before. They usually weren't attacked in their encampment by the creature, but rather when out in hunting parties.

Regardless, he gritted his teeth and did his best to shrug off the effects as much as possible. Through sheer force of will, he was able to crawl towards the birthing tent. One of the midwives had opened the tent flap ever so slightly and was peeking out to see if anything was on its way towards their location, but Konta waved her back in. She caught one glimpse of the torches and seemed to understand the situation, nodding curtly before pulling the tent flap closed as tightly as she could. Konta shoved both the torches into the ground, one on either side of the tent opening, and only stayed long enough to make sure they wouldn't be blown over before starting back towards the bonfire.

Trying to fight back the nausea and the whirling sensation was much harder than he had imagined it would be, especially while trying to keep his eye open for the Gremlins. A couple of times he caught sight of one, but a gust of wind would pick up and it'd be gone again with the flurry.

Konta had just turned a corner and caught sight of the bonfire when he could no longer support his own weight and fell to his side, right on the injured shoulder. He felt no pain from landing on his wound, but relief was the farthest thing from his mind. His whole body had gone numb. One of the villagers rushed to his side, but his vision swam too much to make out who it was.

What he did see was something that tied a knot in his stomach. Another gale had swept through the camp, and now standing in the center of the village near the bonfire was the largest Snow Gremlin he had ever seen. Though he couldn't make out any details, he didn't have to see clearly to tell it had to be at least twenty heads high, its arms stuck out awkwardly as it simply swayed in place. Many of the villagers had congregated in the village center to try and protect each other, and they all now froze in terror at the sight of this great behemoth that towered over them all. Konta could only stare weakly at the Gremlin and wait for whatever it had in store for them.

Out of the corner of his eye, a sudden movement near the fire caught his attention. Blinking rapidly, he managed to focus his sight enough to see that a young hunter he knew as Jaka had rushed to the stone basin still sitting on the fire, full of near boiling water. Zanzu, who had been standing nearby, was so shocked by the young man's actions that he had no time to react as the hunter, grimacing in pain as the hot stone burned his arms, flung the steaming contents at the giant creature.

What happened next was too bizarre for Konta to comprehend completely. The creature began screeching wildly as the water made contact, steam pouring from its body – that was expected. What wasn't expected was the creature breaking into large frozen chunks where the water touched it, while the rest of its body seemed to disintegrate into a snowstorm that quickly blew away while continuing to chitter.

The whole of the village stared on in confusion at the strange turn of events, and it ended up being Konta who made the first move as he tried to force himself to his feet so he could examine the situation better. The poison was still incapacitating him too much to move on his own, but Zanzu seemed to understand what he was attempting. In a few strides he was able to close the distance, hoist Konta up, and help him over to where the icy blocks that were once the Snow Gremlin now sat.

At first glance, it appeared that several large snowflakes had been trapped inside the ice, but as Zanzu lifted a particularly large chunk with his massive hand and brought it close for both of them to see, it dawned on Konta that the snowflakes were, in fact, small bat-like creatures. The more Konta stared at these strange, tiny beasts, the more he started to understand the seemingly impossible mysteries that had surrounded the Snow Gremlin until now: a colony of tiny flying creatures with white fur would easily be able to hide in a snowstorm, striking at unsuspecting prey individually with their tiny fangs. The way Konta's wound was still bleeding slightly made him suspect that whatever venom was in its fangs was not only designed to slow down potential prey, but to keep injuries from clotting so it was easier for the creatures to feed.

The question Konta still held onto was why these small creatures would come together to create the illusion of being some large monster, as they had earlier? Was it some sort of mechanism to try and scare away potential predators? He knew of some animals that would swell up when they sensed danger in order to intimidate possible enemies, but doing so in such an odd manner as the Snow Gremlin did was something he had never seen before.

The next several hours were mostly dedicated to treating the injured, since there had been no real damage to the encampment itself. Konta was grateful to notice that after the initial heavy dizzy spell, he recovered from the poison's effect on his own rather quickly. The other tribesmen who had been attacked had lost much more blood than Konta and required extensive rest in the medical tent, but it didn't look like anyone was in danger of dying.

Never before had the tribe encountered the Snow Gremlin and fended it off without casualties, and it was all thanks to the quick action of Jaka. Normally a feast would be had in celebration of such an achievement, but Murg seemed opposed to the idea, so Jaka was simply given a night of reprieve from his duties while the other villagers went about their business. Konta could understand where the chief was coming from. No matter how lucky they got this time, the tribe could hardly risk lowering their guard while Winter continued to rage on. The festivities could wait until another time.

As Konta sat at the outskirts of the village, an ever-vigilant eye on the snow covered plains that stretched out beyond him, he marveled at what creatures as small as Snow Gremlins could accomplish because of their numbers. In a way, it was uncannily close to what his tribe did on a daily basis: working together to achieve things that they couldn't do alone. It was a strange sort of comfort to know that in the world they fought against every day, his people weren't the only ones who had to band together to survive.

The Newborn

Konta found it hard to believe that Winter was drawing to an end, after all the dangerous situations and stressful nights he had endured during the season. He had begun to believe that he would never live to see the end of the stark white landscape, the bone-chilling days passing by at a glacial pace, or the omnipresent threat of attack that had more than once come to fruition. Yet, reality began to sink in more firmly as Murg started his usual end-of-season march around the encampment and signaled for families to pack up their belongings, only leaving the essential structures like the medical tent and the communal gazebo still standing; those could be quickly disassembled by the tribe and taken on short notice.

Having no tent of his own to deconstruct, Konta busied himself when he wasn't on guard duty with helping the other families prepare for the migration they were about to undertake. The days had grown mild to the point where he didn't need to wear his thick coverings anymore except in the dead of night, and he relished the feeling of not being weighed down all the time by the clothing as he effortlessly broke down one tepee after the other to try and take his mind off the matter pressing endlessly at the back of his mind.

Even though he would soon be going to sleep to prepare for his last night of watch duty at this settlement, Konta had no qualms about helping as many of his tribesmen get ready as possible. Truth be told, he was ready to do anything in his power to expedite their journey from their desolate camp-site, even if it meant losing out on some much de-served, and needed, sleep. He could feel the eyes of the villagers following him, perhaps amused or in awe, as he moved swiftly from one structure to the next, shrugging off any sign of gratitude lest he al-low himself to get distracted. He only stopped when, as he was breaking down Grim and Grima's tent, he felt two sharp taps on his shoulder. Slightly irritated at the interruption of work, he turned—

—and ran straight into the open arms of Kontala.

It took almost a full minute for Konta to recover from the shock of what was happening. Here was his mate, the one person he had longed to see after all these months of hardship and fatigue, embracing him fully with her face buried in his chest. When he was finally sure that he wasn't dreaming, Konta flung his shaking arms around Kontala with an ex-uberance that would've been unbecoming of most hunters. He had never been a hunter to worry about prim and procedure when it came to these intimate actions, though, and could care less what the others thought as he hugged her so tightly that a few moments later he feared he might have hurt her. Before he realized it, though, she had tightened her embrace with a strength Konta didn't know she possessed.

As he was savoring a bliss he hadn't felt in ages, he felt another two quick taps on the shoulder. It was an odd sight to behold as he attempted to turn and address the newcomer without loosening his hold on Kontala, partially dragging her off her feet in the process. In embarrassment, he quickly loosened his hold, almost forgetting that someone else had been trying to get his attention. Only now did Konta realize that it was Grima, who had been midwifing for Kontala during her birthing. Now an icy shock washed over Konta as he noticed a bundle of cloth that Grima was extending towards him.

His hands trembled uncontrollably as he took the parcel from the tribeswoman, who carefully adjusted his arms so he was properly supporting the right places. From the small opening in the wraps, a tiny face poked out, its eyes closed as it slept in peace. Konta marveled at how tiny and light the baby was, that something so small and precious could ever possibly grow to be a…

With as little rustling as he could manage, Konta unfolded the blankets quickly and took a peek at his baby. A small fire of excitement burst to life inside him: he had his boy.

The other hunters silently laughed, and it took a moment for Konta to realize that he had been grinning at his discovery. He could feel his face flushing as he hurriedly bundled his boy back up and passed him gingerly to Kontala. His humiliation was only matched by the intense joy that coursed through him. His worries had been alleviated, and he finally had the family he had been dreaming about. No amount of embarrassment could possibly dampen his spirits at this moment.

He bustled off to work again, a new energy in his step, but it was only a couple of hours later that Murg approached him and removed his pelt. Konta had been feeling tired, but he didn't think it showed that much. Murg's motives, however, were made more apparent when he placed a hand on his back and led him to the gazebo where Kontala was now sitting and nursing their son. Konta thought he saw the vestiges of a smile behind Murg's grizzled beard before the old chief left to continue attending to the preparations, leaving him with his mate and newborn child.

Now that he stood there, Kontala looking up at him with a soft smile and his boy suckling happily away, new worries and concerns began to bubble to the surface of his mind. His baby was completely defenseless against the threats of the world around him, and Kontala would be devoting all of her time and energy for many seasons to come in order to help their child grow into a strong and capable hunter. Would he be able to protect them both? This last Winter had been the most brutal of any he had lived through before, and there was no reason to believe that they couldn't get worse from here. Was he strong enough to see them through the hardships that lay ahead? Would he be forced to suffer as Bobo had just a few seasons ago and try to cope with the loss of his offspring?

Despite his thoughts, he knew enough by now to not let his fears cross his face, lest he worry Kontala. Instead he lowered himself onto the rug beside the fire where she rested, gently putting one arm around her and gingerly resting his free hand on his son. Of course, he knew the answers to these questions already. He had been struggling for his life, and for the lives of his tribe, for as long as he could remember. Things were no different now than they were before. He would fight on, to the bitter end if need be, to protect himself and everything that was important to him. As if they could sense his unease, Kontala leaned against him at that moment and planted the gentlest of kisses on his cheek, just as Konta's son opened his eyes and looked at his father. It was all the assurance Konta needed that his struggle was worth any amount of suffering down the road.

Looking into his boy's eyes, Konta realized with a start that he had yet to think of a name for him. It took little time for him to come up with one, however. If he was Konta, and his wife was Kontala, then this boy of his would be Kontaren, the babe who would one day succeed his father and walk amongst his tribesmen as a fierce warrior. Just the thought of it filled him with even more passion and determination to see the man his son would one day grow to be.

Konta spent the rest of the day alternating between menial tasks and spending time with his family, finally retreating to one of the few remaining tents to take a nap as the day was winding down. Though he had been given a day of rest, it was his turn for night watch, and regardless of a pardon from Murg he wasn't about to abdicate such an important responsibility.

The darkness bore down heavily on him as he awoke feeling unusually refreshed for a change. The soft sounds of breathing right next to him startled him slightly, but he calmed as his eyes adjusted to the dark and he realized it was only his Kontala and their Kontaren dozing blissfully nearby. He quickly slipped into his clothes and pelt, careful not to wake them as he placed a gentle hand on his mate's shoulder. As he reached for his weapons, he had a sudden urge to grab his hammer alongside his usual spear and knife. Even though it would only slow him down, tonight he decided it would be better to play it safe and made sure the hefty club was strapped to his side before heading off into the cold night.

With Winter's end so close at hand, the tribe had felt bold enough to build a particularly large fire to warm the night patrol, a gesture that Konta was duly grateful for as he quickly washed and warmed himself before bundling up his cloaks. The last thing he wanted to feel on his last night of watch was cold and miserable.

Konta's patrol route took him right alongside the vast cliff face the tribe had huddled against. Even though it was a bit farther than he had to go, Konta marched until he met where the cliff descended and met with the ground, stationing himself there to make sure nothing slipped into the village in the dead of night.

Uneventful minutes passed into uneventful hours as he sat, ever vigilant with spear in one hand and knife in the other. By now the herds of Winter beasts would be migrating towards colder climates with the coming warmth of Spring, and the lack of any predatory sightings by his fellow scouts only further confirmed that the great dangers of the season had likely passed already.

The Moon had crossed most of the sky when Konta first felt a shiver. He hardly paid attention to it until he felt it again moments later. The weather was nowhere near as cold as it had been earlier in the season, and Konta was always careful to bundle up tightly to ward away the chill, so when a third shiver hit him he began to grow concerned. It wasn't until the fourth shiver that he realized it wasn't the cold causing it. Something was shaking the ground.

Immediately Konta leaped to the sloping ground that gave rise to the cliff and ran as quickly and silently as he could to get a better viewpoint. If an earthquake was happening, that was one thing, but if something else was causing these tremors...

Once safely hidden in a shrub several heads above ground level, he was able to take his time and look out towards the horizon. It didn't take long to see the shadow of a shape, silhouetted against the moonlight, slowly lumbering across the vast plains. Konta's heart caught in his throat, and though he begged in his mind for the creature to change direction and be on its way, he knew beyond a shadow of a doubt what it was: a Razorback Mammoth, wandering straight towards the village.

The Razorback Mammoth

Konta's tribe had faced innumerable dangers in his lifetime alone, and obviously far more than those before his time. In this last season alone, they had managed to drive off a Zero Celberus, a herd of Blight Mares, and a swarm of Snow Gremlins – all of which Konta had seen inflict severe damage on their village in the past. Despite all these threats, though, none of those came close in comparison to what a lone Razorback Mammoth could do if left unchecked.

There was no one thing that made the Razorback the veritable king beast of Winter; rather, it was the combination of all its unique characteristics. It was the largest creature that hunted in Winter and, in fact, one of the largest hunting creatures ever discovered by the tribe – only the Tortoasise and Sponge Whale were known to be larger. Unlike the latter, however, the Razorback was incredibly aggressive in nature with little to no provocation, attacking any living creature that strayed across its path. To complement their brute strength and deadly tusks, the Razorback also possessed the singular weapon that gave birth to Konta's namesake for them: a strange fur that froze and solidified in the cold to form long, blade-like tufts that ran across their backs, protecting them from any attacks made where they couldn't reach and, thus, were most vulnerable.

It took Konta a few moments to regain composure once he spotted the beast stumbling across the plains, for it had been hammered into him from an early age to fear the Razorback Mammoth above almost any other creature known to the tribe. Fleeing from one was considered the best course of action, but as he stared at it, unable to look away in fear, he started noticing a few strange things about this particular Mammoth. For one thing, it was undeniably smaller than an adult Razorback; those tended to be twenty heads high, but this one couldn't have been more than ten. It had to be an adolescent. The fact that it was by itself was odd, too, since Razorbacks were pack animals and were rarely encountered by themselves, another point that added to their danger factor.

He immediately considered rushing back to his tribe and raising the alarm, but outrunning even a young Razorback would be difficult at best, and if it saw him in his flight he'd likely be run down before he even got within sight of the village. Instead he decided to stay in his shrubby hiding place and bide his time just a short while longer.

The beast lumbered closer still to his location, but Konta was still confident, if a little uneasy, that he was completely concealed. The waning Moon cast only a soft light over the plains, not nearly enough to reflect off his pelt and betray his location. Still, he knew there wasn't much time to figure out how to handle the situation.

Konta couldn't tell how long it would take the creature to reach the village at its current rate, but even at its lumbering pace, it would likely make it there before Sunrise, and most of the hunters right now were either asleep or on patrol elsewhere. There would be little stopping the Razorback if it began a rampage.

It was at that instant that a wild decision popped into Konta's mind. He knew he couldn't outrace the beast, and by now it would certainly see him if he tried to bolt for the village. Even sticking to the slope where it would be slow to reach him, eventually the cliff would rise sharply and he'd be unable to descend safely. There was only one way at this point that Konta could prevent the Razorback Mammoth from wreaking complete havoc on his people.

He would have to face it alone.

The idea curdled his insides and made him retch, but there really wasn't any other choice. If he didn't stop the Razorback's progress now, it would stumble its way right into the camp, unless it made a radical change in direction soon – a risk that was too heavy to gamble on. Trying to run for the village would only lead it there faster, and he would be sighted anyways. He had to attempt to fight it now, even if that prospect was basically suicide. He only hoped that in the struggle, he could make enough noise to alert the tribe and prepare them for what was headed their way.

Konta took a deep breath, trying to stave off the urge to vomit and calm the intense shaking that rocked his body. When he finally steadied himself as much as he could, he stood from the bush and shouted at the beast with all his might.

The roar of defiance he unleashed surprised even him, so unaccustomed was he to the sound of his own voice. The Mammoth was also apparently taken aback, for it let out a great trumpeting sound and reared back on its hind legs in defense from the sudden challenge. That, at least, gave Konta a slight feeling of satisfaction: let the beast warn anything in the area that it was near, he thought. No other predator would dare wander towards the cry of a Razorback Mammoth willingly, and it might have been loud enough in the dead of night to carry all the way to the village.

As the monster lowered back to all fours, shaking the earth beneath its feet, both of its beady eyes locked onto Konta. With another screeching trumpet, it began to stampede towards Konta. Still, the hunter held some high ground, and it would take some effort for the Mammoth to reach him.

He began to run the opposite direction of the village as fast as his legs would carry him. For a moment he thought of charging up the cliff side and possibly trying to coax the beast into falling off the edge, but more likely than not it would simply force him over the side. Instead, he opted to aggravate the creature as he ran, hoping its cries would be heard by his tribe. As he ran, he continually snatched rocks from the ground and lobbed them over his head at the Razorback. Though not nearly enough to injure the creature, it did let out several more trumpets of anger as it picked up speed.

Konta knew this plan wouldn't last long. Already the Mammoth had closed more than half the distance between them, and he had barely covered much ground. The ground shook more with each step closer the beast became, making running a doubly difficult effort. To compound all this, his body felt unnaturally heavy and ungainly, and now he cursed inward as he realized that the hammer hanging from his waist was only slowing him down. He was about to untie it and fling it aside when a deafening roar sounded right behind him.

With no time to think, Konta clenched his spear tightly and whirled around, stabbing out as he flung himself to the side. His blow struck true, and the fire hardened point of the spit dug into the beast's flesh as it barreled past him, unable to quickly slow from its charge. Konta hit the ground in a roll, the footfalls of the Mammoth so heavy that the trembling ground bounced the hunter against his will several times. Konta winced as he was dashed against some loose stones uncontrollably, the feeling of fresh cuts and bruises beginning to well up all over his body.

Finally he managed to steady himself, and quickly rose to his feet gasping as he took quick note of his strike. The spear still hung loosely from the Mammoth's side, but for all the good it had done, it might as well have been a pinprick. The creature trumpeted in fury as it shook itself and almost effortlessly dislodged the spear, with hardly a trickle of blood to mark that it had been wounded at all.

The next pass would be the last one. Even with his adrenaline rushing, he knew that he wouldn't be able to dodge a second time. He was still winded from his flight, and though he wasn't gravely injured, he knew that his movements would be hindered too much to leap out of the way in time. His only remaining option was to try and leave some lasting impact on the beast, to try and injure it enough that it would either retreat where it came from or at least be less of a threat should it find his village after it was done with him.

The ground shook as the Razorback Mammoth started for him again, its tusks poised to skewer the hunter where he stood panting. His knife was all but useless, a tool used for precision cuts to vital points that wouldn't do any good against the thick hide of his impending death. Instinctively, his hand closed around the shaft of his last remaining option. As the tip of the Mammoth's tusk loomed within inches of Konta's face he swung upwards, putting every last ounce of strength he could muster into his hammer blow.

There was a loud splintering sound and a great crack as the tusk broke where the hammerhead connected. The point of the tusk was thrust upward, but the tip of it still grazed Konta's left eye and sent him sprawling to the ground. His head swam with pain as he felt the blood pour from the gash in his face, and he expected to feel the crushing finality of the Razorback's foot trod down on him, but all that came was the horrific bellow of pain from the beast. He could feel its colossal foot crash down just next to him, and realizing he was still alive for the moment, he quickly gathered his wits to now see that in its anguish and anger the Razorback had reared onto its hind legs. Its left tusk had broken clear away, and the pain had been enough to stop the creature in its tracks. Any second now, though, it would regain its senses and undoubtedly come crashing down on him.

A strange feeling stole over Konta as he looked up at his imminent demise silhouetted against the Moonlit sky. He felt a bizarre catharsis at the sight of the marred animal, knowing that if he had to go out, at least he had done something far greater than he had ever hoped. He had injured a Razorback Mammoth by himself. The creature seemed to hover over him, slowly descending to crush him, but he had already accepted death as his thoughts turned back to his tribe.

He found himself wishing it had been Zanzu who had come this way tonight. He had killed a Razorback by himself before and could have probably handled this far better than Konta. He thought of his fellow hunters Klik and Grim, Tamto and Senga, his old friend Faygo, now long deceased. He thought of all the hunts that he had survived before and wished that any of his fellow tribesmen had been here to see his last stand. More than anything, though, he thought of Kontala and their newborn Kontaren, whom he would never get to see grow into a hunter.

He didn't realize it, but his body had been moving on its own. Without a single thought put into it, his hands reached for the broken Mammoth tusk that lay where it had fallen next to him and pulled it upright, pointed straight at its former owner.

What transpired over the next few seconds blurred together for Konta. As he knelt with his arms wrapped around the tusk, he could feel the full weight of the Mammoth bear down and halt disturbingly. The beast let out a gurgling, almost pitiable noise as it landed unsteadily on its feet, where it only stood for a fraction of a moment before teetering sideways. One of its legs clipped Konta, knocking him down and sending his vision reeling again. When he finally managed to steady himself, he rose on shaky, aching legs. Right next to him laid the motionless body of the Mammoth, blood steadily bubbling from around the edges of where the tusk had stuck straight through its heart. It took a few moments for Konta to comprehend what he had just managed to do, but for some reason it didn't seem to matter much. The beast was dead: that was all that mattered.

His head was still swimming, but somehow he found the strength to start back towards the village. He took little care in concealing his movements. He had already given himself up for dead and was physically and mentally exhausted. It made little difference to him if something else showed up at that time to finish what the Razorback had started.

Konta barely noticed the sky slowly brightening, the Sun creeping up over the distant trees that had begun to stretch upward to welcome the coming Spring. He didn't notice the slight smell as he passed over the invisible territory line the tribe had laid out to try and ward off predators. He didn't pick up his pace as the tents of his people rose before him, nor did he stop walking when hunters and tribeswomen started rushing out from the tents towards him. It was only when a large form blocked his path and took hold of his shoulders that he finally stopped moving his feet, looking up to see Zanzu looking at him with an expression of complete bewilderment.

He looked around, seeing faces but not being able to put the names he came up with to any of them. Dimly, he realized that his body felt wet. He looked down at himself to see that he was covered in blood, most likely his own. A glance over his shoulder revealed a small trail of droplets that he had been shedding during his march back. He normally would've worried about it leading a predator back to the village, but like just about everything else it didn't matter at this moment.

Konta shrugged off Zanzu, who oddly obliged as Konta continued walking until he finally caught sight of Kontala rushing forward, her eyes bulging with fear and worry as she clutched tightly to Kontaren. He stopped, teetering in place, and looked at them both.

Then he smiled, and his legs gave out under him as everything went black.

* * *

The first thing Konta felt was something moist being pressed against the left side of his face. He tried to open his eyes, but could only manage to crack open the right one, and even that simple action caused his head to explode in pain. Still, he could dimly make out the face of his mate looking back at him, her expression surprised. It seemed he was lying outside on a rug, because past Kontala all he could see was a vast expanse of blue sky. He forced himself to sit, causing more pain to wrack his body, but there were more important things to worry about at the moment. How long had he been out? Had there been an attack on the village after his careless mistake of leaving a trail?

He saw now that he had been laid out near the communal tent where the fire pit had been dug. It didn't take him long to notice that something large had been dragged into the village and was now sitting just outside the tent: the body of the Razorback Mammoth he had killed.

Sitting had been painful, but standing was practically tortuous. It felt as if every bone in his body had been broken. Konta felt unusually stiff, noticing quickly that his body was almost completely covered in bandages and poultices. He reached toward the wrapping on his face that covered his left eye, only to remember the blow he had suffered from the Mammoth. He likely didn't have an eye left there. Kontala had tried to keep him from moving, but he fought until she finally gave up with a sigh of resignation. After standing still for a little bit to make sure he could keep himself upright, he slowly shuffled out towards where the body lay.

Many of the villagers had gathered around the corpse, where they either prodded at it gingerly as if afraid it might still be alive, or otherwise simply stared awestruck at it. Several parents had to strike their pups when they wandered towards its back, the bladed fur as dangerous as ever. Konta could understand their interest. It was extremely rare to have a chance to see a Razorback up close, as the last one killed by the tribe was back when Zanzu had returned with the trophy he now wore as a pelt.

Two taps alighted on his shoulder, and Konta turned to meet the Chief's gaze. Murg looked at him, appraising for a moment, then nodded and took Konta by the arm and dragged him away from the crowd. It took some time, as Konta could still barely move faster than a limp, but eventually he was led into the Chief's tent, where a couple of tribeswomen ushered them through the flaps before stepping out, leaving the two hunters alone.

Murg turned to Konta and stared into his eye for a good long while. Whatever he was looking for, the hunter couldn't fathom, but finally the Chief turned and went to a woven basket that sat at the far end of the tent. Murg rummaged through it for a bit, closed the basket, and walked back to Konta, shoving something in his hand. Konta sucked in a deep breath as he saw that he was holding the sleeve bracelet that he had coveted for so long – the sign of Murg's favor. Konta had finally been accepted as one of the top hunters.

Before he could put it on, though, Murg grabbed Konta's arm and held it out. Konta watched in curiosity as the Chief reached to his own pelt and plucked off one of the numerous ashen-colored feathers that covered it. Before he could react, Murg stabbed him with the quill and held it in place. Konta winced by reflex, but strangely the pinion sticking into his flesh didn't hurt. Instead, he felt a soft warmth begin to radiate through his body, and he watched in amazement as the feather's ash coloring flared to a fiery reddish gold. Ever so slowly, some of the down began to smolder away, and as it did, the pain flowing through Konta dissipated, replaced with the warmth that had been coursing through him. As the last of his pain subsided, the golden feather slowly faded back to grey, and Murg took the bracelet from him, wrapping it around the feather and tightly securing it to his arm.

Konta was completely confused as to what had just happened. He flexed his arms a couple times, as if testing to see if the pain would return. When he was sure that he was fine, he discarded the wrappings that he had been wearing before, and looking at his body he saw that the bruises and gashes he had suffered from his fight with the Razorback Mammoth were gone, without so much as the faintest scar to suggest they had ever been there in the first place. He remembered his injured eye and removed the bandage on his head full of hope, but when he tried to open his eye he realized with a heavy heart that only scarred tissue remained there. It seemed that the healing feather couldn't heal an eye already lost.

Still, Konta now had answers to questions he had been pondering before, as well as a host of new questions. He understood how Faygo had managed to heal so quickly after their fight with the Ravagers during Autumn, but if he had managed to heal from that, why did he die to the Rafflesion? Did the burning of the feather mean that it had limited healing power? He understood that the bracelet Murg gave him now was to hide that he had the feather, but why would the Chief hide the fact that he had such an incredible tool at his disposal? Wouldn't he want to give this to every hunter, to decrease risk of death during the hunt?

As if to confirm his suspicion, Murg grabbed Konta's sleeved arm and put a single finger to his lips.

This was to be a secret between Konta, the Chief, and those who also bore the bracelet; there was no question there. Konta nodded in understanding, and Murg gave the hunter one of his rare smiles that shone even through the bushy tangle of beard the wizened tribal chief wore.

With Spring so close, the village felt safe enough to hold a feast that night in celebration of the end of Winter, and more so, Konta's incredible hunting trophy. Though food stores were never terribly plentiful at Winter's close, there had been enough successful hunts that all the villagers were allowed to eat to their heart's content, and though it had been young, the Razorback Mammoth still had ample meat on its body to hold the tribe over until more bountiful Spring hunts replenished their stock.

As was custom, Konta was offered the first piece of the Mammoth meat, a sign of his triumph over the beast. He stared down at the still sizzling slab and knew what would follow: the hide had already been stripped from the carcass, and over the next few days the tribeswomen would fashion it into a pelt that Konta would wear as his new symbol of status amongst the hunters. In essence, he would hold the same stature as Zanzu, which would effectively make him the second Head Hunter of the tribe. It was an honor that every hunter aspired to.

After what felt like ages of staring at the piece of meat, feeling the eyes of the tribe watching and waiting for him to partake of his kill, Konta stood and flung the slab of Mammoth into the communal fire.

The hunters and tribeswomen looked at him, then at each other, confusion spreading like wildfire across their faces. They then watched as Konta strode to just outside the tent, where the Razorback's hide lay folded. He picked it up carefully, lest he cut himself on its spines (and raise suspicion at them suddenly healing), dragged it to the fire, and tossed it in too.

Several hunters now rose from their seats, a mixture of shock, anger, and puzzlement crossing their faces. Konta didn't care, though, and when Zanzu stood and pulled them back into their seats, they didn't refuse. Nobody was foolish enough to argue with the Head Hunter's commands.

Konta walked away from the feast, wondering if his decision was the right one. He used to dream of one day becoming Head Hunter and leading the tribe into an age of prosperity. Being the best hunter he could be was always the goal he strove to accomplish, but he had been thinking a lot that day about what it really meant to be a hunter, and what the pelt he wore really represented. The Razorback Mammoth that died by his hands was only a juvenile, and after having looked at its body more closely earlier in the day, he realized it had been half starved to death before he encountered it. It was only through a fluke chance that he had managed to kill the beast, not some great act of cunning that the tribe likely thought had transpired. If he wore its pelt, Konta felt it would've been an affront to every hunter who put himself in mortal peril to prove their worth to the tribe.

He wandered into the tent Kontala, Kontaren, and he were using and pulled out his Obsidian Panther pelt, which he wasn't wearing during his "recovery" from his injuries. Folded inside it was the sparkling stone that once made up the head of his hammer. The hammer's shaft had broken when he struck the Razorback's tusk, but the precious stone that made his hammer so special had been recovered with the corpse of the beast.

The Panther pelt and the hammerhead, both of these were trophies that Konta had once felt he had gotten through blind luck too. Now, though, he realized just how important to him they were to his identity. He felt they were inseparable parts of who he was, and knew now what being a real hunter truly was to him: it was the strength to protect the tribe, and more importantly, protect his mate and their pup.

He sat for a long while, staring at the cowl of his pelt that still retained the aspect of the beast it was created from, locked in a perpetual snarling expression. At some point in the night, Kontala came into the tent with Kontaren in her arms and sat next to him. She rested her head on his shoulder and stared at the pelt with him as she nursed their son. She rested one hand gently on his arm, and Konta knew that she understood his feelings, somehow, just like she always did. Konta felt Kontala's breathing grow slow and steady, knowing that she had fallen asleep where she sat, but he sat up looking at the pelt all through that last night of Winter.

In that one small tent was everything in the world that Konta held closest to his heart. It was for these things that he was, and always would be, a hunter.

Flashback: The Obsidian Panther (1)

Konta awoke with a start. His breathing came in short, spastic gasps and a thin coat of cold sweat streaked his brow. As he tried to slow his rapidly beating heart, he struggled to recall what had led to him feeling this way: it was definitely a dream, but what had happened in it? Try as he might, he couldn't recall, and as the seconds dragged on he felt more and more foolish for being so distraught over nothing.

Still, he couldn't shake the uneasy feeling that seemed to cling to his bare shoulders as he rose from his pallet. Around him his fellow hunters were asleep and, from the look of it, far more soundly than Konta had been. It wasn't unusual for Konta to rise before the others, but for once he felt a pang of jealousy that he couldn't rest a bit longer like they were.

Carefully, Konta navigated his way over the prone bodies to the corner of the tent where he kept his equipment. Just like every other day, he strapped on his loincloth, his flint knife sheath, and his chest belt that secured a spear to his back. He was tempted to bring the hammer he had recently assembled from the strong glittering stone he had found, but was still unaccustomed to its weight and so left it where it lay.

Even going through the usual motions, though, the dread from his nightmare followed him outside the tent as he headed to wash up at the communal basin. He wished that he had a pelt to drape across his back, as if it would be enough to shield him from his baseless fears, but he had yet to prove himself worthy of one in a hunt. Hopefully, today would give him a chance to remedy that problem.

The horizon was barely tinted with orange at this time of the morning, and the sky still hung heavy with stars as he splashed near boiling water from the basin on his face in a final effort to wash away his strange feelings. When that proved fruitless, he gave a soft sigh and wandered off to where the tribeswomen were preparing breakfast.

As he piled random fruits and preserved meats into his arms, out of the corner of his eye he caught three of the younger tribeswomen looking at him. Two of them were wearing smiles he didn't like: it was the type of condescending smile flowering tribeswomen who were ready to find a mate gave to uninitiated hunters like him, as if questioning his capability to provide for the tribe. The third one also gave him a smile, but it was much softer and accompanied with an even softer blush, and when her gaze met his she turned away hastily. Konta took note of her long, bushy hair that fell past her shoulders to her waist and the almost endearing way she tried to hide behind it. She was a little smaller than most of the other young tribeswomen, but Konta found himself oddly charmed by that. He knew he would have to keep an eye out for her in the future.

By the time he was finished with his breakfast, most of the other hunters from the tribe had finally risen and were in preparation for the day ahead. The older hunters were donning their various animal cloaks as they washed or ate or honed their weapons, while the other uninitiated hunters like himself broke off into small groups to either tend to various chores around the camp or to prepare for the hunts the veterans would be taking them on today.

Konta milled in with the latter, trying to find the few other boys he had been assigned to meet with the day prior. As he looked around intently, something thudded on his shoulder hard, but when he turned it was only the grinning face of Faygo, his friend he'd known since he was old enough to remember. Normally, Konta never bothered putting a name to a tribesman who wasn't a full-fledged hunter, but Faygo was different. Konta had given him that name long before Faygo's recent kill of the Triceraboar, and when his friend had shared part of the kill with him that night it made Konta realize how much he meant to Faygo as well. He hoped one day his pups could be just as good friends with Faygo's.

Today, though, they would have to go their separate ways. Faygo gave Konta one last friendly punch on the shoulder before jogging off to meet up with Bren, one of the older hunters in the tribe. Konta was a bit jealous that he couldn't be part of that group: the young hunters all revered the older hunters, who had to be very skilled to have lived so long, and none came close to Bren's age. Even with his White Wolf pelt draped over his shoulders, Bren's gray hair peeked out from the hood of his cowl. Konta mused for a moment that his father might have been as old as Bren if he were still alive, but the thought was short lived. The living tribe always came before the dead.

Finally Konta was able to track down the small group of young hunters he was to be part of. To his surprise, they were standing next to a group of full-fledged hunters that equaled their number. He was able to pick out Varsa, with his Boallista pelt wrapped oddly around his shoulders, the snake's head perched in a perpetual hiss on his shoulder. Next to Varsa was Telku, who wore a pelt woven from the hides of multiple small, black-quilled beasts Konta recognized as Coalcupines, though he had only seen pictures of living ones. Finally, behind those two was a small, squat hunter that Konta knew was normally a nocturnal scout, the one he referred to as Kukin. Like Telku, Kukin's pelt was made of several smaller creatures lashed together, but his were even more impressive, because Kukin's pelt was made of three Canteen Turtles. The sight sent a shiver down Konta's spine. It was only a couple Summers' passing since the failed scouting expedition he had been part of where the hunter Sinje had perished, along with several of Konta's fellow fledgling hunters. Clearly Kukin was a skilled hunter if he was able to capture three of a Tortoasise's brood and escape alive.

The other hunting parties going out today only had one seasoned hunter with them, so Konta was beyond curious about why their party in particular had thrice that number. Kukin, the apparent leader of the group, gave an approving nod when he saw Konta approach and motioned for the hunters to head out at once. Konta's heart raced excitedly at the prospect of what lay ahead, and for the first time that morning his feeling of dread was forgotten.

Their party passed by the hunters who had guard duty today, and Konta couldn't help but notice how many more sentries seemed to be watching the outskirts than usual. Usually during Spring every hunter that could be spared was busy hunting or training the fledglings, taking advantage of the calm climate and more docile prey. On the other hand, Konta couldn't ever remember the tribe settling in this area during Spring. Perhaps the dangers in these parts were greater than he knew?

As was usual for Spring, the land was lush with green, leafy plant life that made it much easier for the party to travel conspicuously. As it turned out, Kukin's leadership was a well-made decision, for

Konta's hunting party found itself stopping and making camp for several days afterward rather than returning to the settlement. The excitement and fear was almost too much to bear for young Konta, who had never spent the night so far from the tribe before, but Kukin was no stranger to this situation. He never seemed to need to sleep, oftentimes slipping off in the dark – scouting ahead, Konta assumed – and his Canteen Turtle pelt let him hold more than enough water to keep the party well slaked even as natural water sources started to wane. Varsa and Telku were no slouches either, quickly reacting to even the slightest warning and ushering the young ones to safety, more than once allowing them to narrowly avoid dangers from natural traps and nocturnal predators.

On the fourth day out, Kukin suddenly commanded them to stop their march. Ahead, Konta could see the thick foliage of trees and shrubs they had been winding through came to an abrupt end. The scout motioned for the fledglings to take to the trees and spot ahead, which Konta was happy to oblige. After so many days of only watching the other hunters work, he was eager to get some experience for himself. Konta chose the tallest tree he could find and navigated his way up deftly but carefully, lest he draw unwanted attention or wake up something. At the top, though, the sight that Konta surveyed made his breath catch in his throat, and he almost let go of the leafy fronds he clung to.

Just ahead of where the party had stopped there was a shallow grassy valley where a small herd of some large, indistinguishable beasts appeared to be grazing. Undoubtedly, this was what their hunting party had set out to capture, but to his right, towards where the Sun had begun to descend, a stark black expanse of desert and rocky outcroppings could be seen. The surface of this bleak area shimmered in the sunlight, and even from such a distance Konta could feel the baking heat the land radiated.

Even though Konta had been on innumerable hunts since his youth, never once had he laid eyes on the area he came to know as the Blacklands. Normally, the tribe kept well away from the area, where nourishment and shelter was nearly impossible to come by and terrible predators conditioned to live in the harsh environment roamed year round. Before, Konta had only seen pictures of the Blacklands and the various beasts that inhabited it, but for a moment the young hunter was enthralled by its dark, desolate beauty. Konta was reminded of Telku and his pelt; Coalcupines were one of the creatures Konta knew to live in the Blacklands, and for a moment he felt a great surge of respect for his elder who had hunted in such a terrible area. He pondered what other sorts of beasts could possibly survive in such a wasteland. Surely a pelt from such prey would be an incredible achievement and cement a position as a mighty hunter in the tribe.

Konta quickly recollected his thoughts as he skipped back down the tree, knowing that today he had to keep focused on the task at hand. At the bottom he reconvened with the veteran hunters and his fledgling brethren, recapping what he had seen with a couple deft hand signals: a herd of beasts straight ahead, and a point in the direction of the Blacklands with the signal for danger. The other three fledglings gave the same report, and Kukin gave an approving nod. He obviously knew what the situation was already and was simply testing to see if his wards had observed the same.

Telku led the hunters ahead slowly, right up to where the forest began to thin and the ground sloped into the valley. At the bottom was the herd that Konta saw before, slowly meandering along and grazing every so often. At this distance, Konta could clearly see that it was a group of about seven Nuevenceratops: massive scaly herbivores that boasted nine deadly horns on the crests atop their heads. Five of them appeared to be adults, their powerful bodies as large as two of the tribe's tents lashed together, but two smaller whelps straggled near the back of the herd. One only had five horns on its head, while the smaller of the two had only three, marking them as far from adulthood.

It was the two whelps that Telku and Varsa motioned towards. Varsa climbed into the tallest nearby tree and began to unwind his Boallista pelt while the other two veterans each took two of the fledglings and began to reposition in the forest. Konta, who was assigned with Kukin, already could see what the plan of attack was: strike from a distance to panic the herd, drive the whelps as far away from the parents as possible, then strike for the kill against them.

If things went well, they could drive the parents far away enough to grab the whelp and make off with it whole bodied; should the parents decide to stick around and fight back, though, they might only be able to take what they could cut off the carcass. Even a young Nuevenceratops had a lot of meat, though, and that would be a boon in the coming seasons for the tribe.

Once both hunter teams were in position, Kukin pulled out a small piece of shiny material and shone it in the direction Konta knew Varsa was in. After a couple of tense seconds, there was a loud *twang* sound and something green shot from the treetops at a blinding speed. It struck the leg of the larger whelp with pinpoint accuracy, sticking to the terrified creature as it began to holler loudly and run around in panicked circles. The adults, now sensing danger, quickly tried to usher the whelps to the safety of the trees on the far side, but the one struck by Varsa ignored its parents as it ran off in agony. To the luck of the hunters, the parents appeared to have given up the injured one as a lost cause and loped away with the other two in tow, leaving the now injured juvenile to fend for itself.

Once the rest of the herd had vanished, the two hunter parties descended silently in tandem, spears and knives brandished to deliver a quick kill. As they ran down the hill, Konta suddenly felt the chill he had experienced earlier that day, stronger than ever. He tried to shake it off, but this time it wouldn't go away. Something in his gut was telling him to get out of here as fast as possible, but he forced himself forward regardless.

That was when he heard the snarl.

From the top of the hill just across from where Konta and the hunters were descending, three long ebony shapes rocketed towards the injured Nuevenceratops. The unfortunate herbivore barely had time to let out a shriek of dismay before the shapes pounced, flashing claws and teeth longer than Konta's finger. He froze for a moment, transfixed at the sight of the trio of predators, and could feel the cold sweat beading on his brow as he recognized them as Obsidian Panthers.

The pictures he had seen did no justice to the feral majesty the giant cats exuded. Their eyes glistened a deep green, like rare gemstones marred only by the single black slit that divided each in two. Their impossibly black coats shone in the midday Sun, so fine that Konta had no doubt that they were in fact made of the glassy rock he had derived the Panther's name from. Even as they attacked their scaly prey, there was an eerie grace to the teamwork the Panthers employed to swiftly down the Nuevenceratops – two targeted the ankles to hinder it before the third struck at the throat for the kill.

The other hunters had barely stopped running by the time the small glaring of cats had finished the job. As he stood there, numb with fear, Konta realized that it had been strange for the herd of Nuevenceratops to leave their whelp to die so easily. Surely they had only left when they caught the scent of the Obsidian Panthers. Now, Konta was wishing that he had heeded that feeling he had been nursing before.

The Panthers started sinking their teeth into the carcass with no hesitation, and for one tiny moment Konta hoped beyond all hope that the hunters would be ignored and they could simply leave. It only took a moment for that hope to be dashed as the pack raised their heads together and took in the sight of the hunting party, as if they only just realized they had had competition for their kill. Slowly, their lips pulled back in angry, silent snarls, their long yellow-ish fangs still stained with blood.

One of the fledglings tossed his spear aside and immediately tried to bolt. He made it about four paces before the nearest Panther closed the distance in a single pounce, its claws sinking into the young hunter's back as he went down with a scream.

The horrid cry jolted the other hunters into action, taking off at a sprint without any thought as to where they were going. Konta knew the jungle would be the best place to try and lose their tail, but with so much open field, the jungle might as well have been a day away. He'd never make it before he was taken down.

A strange yelp came from behind him, and against his better judgment he turned to look as he ran. One of the Panthers had taken off after them, only to tread on a number of large black quills that Telku had dropped from his pelt in his flight. The preda-tor snarled in rage and pain as it lay helpless on the ground, staining the grass around it with a growing pool of blood.

The other two hesitated in front of the Coalcupine blockade, wary of suffering the same fate as their sibling, but by the time the hunters started scrambling up the side of the hill towards the thicket of trees, the remaining Panthers had gotten over their fear and vaulted the barrier, bearing down on them quickly.

Konta managed to get into the trees when he heard another terrible scream behind him. This time he didn't look, but he could tell the cry of another human in agony when he heard it. At this point he could only hope that the Panthers' new victim would slow them down a bit, even while feeling sick at the thought of using his fellow tribesmen as decoys.

Konta's adrenaline forced him onward through the thick brush, not caring how much noise he made or attention he attracted. All he knew was that death was on his trail and stopping for anything was surer to kill him than the possible danger that lay ahead. He ignored the pain of tree branches and prickly bushes raking across his skin as he bolted past them, weaving frantically between the foliage in a desperate attempt to try and shake off his pursuers.

Before long the trees began to thin again, but Konta didn't dare risk turning towards where the plant life grew more plentiful and instead forced himself onward. His vision was half obscured by sweat pouring down his brow and half from sheer terror, but he could see that the area was beginning to darken. Had he really been running so long that night had overtaken him? He had lost all track of time in his mad dash for safety.

Finally, Konta stopped, though only because his body couldn't take the stress anymore. He collapsed to his knees and almost cried out as his legs began to burn. Jumping to his feet, Konta furiously rubbed the sweat from his eyes and took a good look around. His legs began to shake uncontrollably as he took in the looming shapes of massive rock formations surrounding him in every direction, all darker than night and shimmering in the early evening Sun. His legs had carried him straight into the Blacklands.

And he didn't have to turn and look to know what was snarling right behind him.

Flashback: The Obsidian Panther (2)

Beads of sweat continued to trickle down Konta's brow as he slowly drew his dagger from the sheath at his side, desperately fighting to control his heaving breath. It was unlikely he'd be able to strike down the Panther before it spilled his innards with its razor-like claws, but he knew he had to at least try. He pivoted as slowly as he could, trying to avoid aggravating the creature into an attack before he would have a chance to react.

Instead, what he found was a bedraggled beast that was also panting in a desperate attempt to right itself after the chase. Apparently, it had taken a wound or two from one of the other hunters, though which one Konta couldn't tell. However, there was no mistaking the broken wooden spear lodged in the Panther's shoulder or the gashes on its side that looked suspiciously like knife wounds.

Even injured, though, Konta didn't favor his chances against his foe. It was all he could do to keep his hand steady as he held his knife in front of himself, hoping that he'd be able to react to any sudden movements from the Panther.

The beast let out another throaty growl and began advancing slowly towards its prey. Konta instinctively backed up, making sure not to break eye contact lest his momentary lapse in concentration be his last mistake. He gave a halfhearted swipe of his knife towards the Obsidian Panther, but the creature barely flinched at the attack, responding instead with a louder snarl and a swipe of its paw, three claws extended that seemed to make mockery of Konta's weapon. The longest claw barely grazed his chest yet opened a large gash across his front, a testament to their sharpness. Still the beast did not pounce; perhaps it was too injured to attempt it, or otherwise it was more wary of the hunter than he had expected.

Step by step Konta retreated, until suddenly forced to stop when his back hit something solid. He would've startled if his attention hadn't been absolutely focused on the Panther. Instead, he stood with his back to the wall, knife still poised at the ready. The Obsidian Panther halted at a few paces distance and, to Konta's shock, laid down. For a few tense moments Konta stared at it, rigid as stone, but all the Panther did was rest its head on its paws and stare at him. Finally, Konta risked breaking eye contact to take the briefest glance around, all while continuing to hold his knife out.

The rocky outcropping he had backed into wasn't terribly large. The top of the ridge could be reached if he stretched for it, and a few strides in either direction the obsidian formation opened up to barren, blackened plains. Behind the Panther, the jungle that Konta had been running through could just barely be seen in the distance. The problem Konta faced was figuring out which direction to travel in order to get back to the village. The Sun had already set, and though there was still some dim twilight lingering, the way it reflected off the Blacklands made it impossible to tell which direction was which. He'd have to wait until daybreak before he would have a point of reference to travel. That was the least of his problems though, considering the vicious animal still lying right before him and the fact that in short time it would be too dark for him to see anything, especially in a landscape that mirrored the night sky.

Konta was still confused at why the Obsidian Panther would lay down when he still held his weapon at the ready. Just to test the waters, he leaned forward and raised his knife the slightest bit. Without a moment's hesitation the Panther's lips curled back and it hissed, snapping its teeth slightly in warning. Konta pulled back, perhaps too quickly, as his empty left hand slid along a nearby rock and was cut wide open. He winced, but willed himself to keep his guard up. It was his own foolish mistake; Konta knew very well that obsidian cleaved easily and was razor sharp, but he had completely forgotten in this situation that the dangerous rock surrounded him on all sides. He was effectively hemmed in on all sides by blades, with a living mass of them lounging right in front of him.

The adrenaline coursing endlessly through Konta's body helped him stave off exhaustion as the night slowly passed. Now the Panther seemed to be dozing, though its eyes never fully closed and shot open if Konta made any sudden movements. On rare occasions it would raise its head and glance over its shoulder, taking a sniff or two before returning to rest, but even with its attention diverted, Konta didn't dare try to attack. Though he had managed to dress his bleeding hand with a strip of his loincloth, the wound still stung without mercy. Between that and the gash on his chest, all the lost blood was beginning to make him lightheaded. Any attempt to kill the Panther would likely be clumsy (and fatal), so instead he bid his time in hope that the creature would fall asleep and let him slink away.

Thankfully, the night was much brighter than he had expected, in part due to the Moon's light reflecting off the shiny surface of the Blacklands and lighting all of Konta's surroundings. In the dead of night, the Blacklands had a haunting, quiet beauty that Konta, despite his imminent danger, couldn't help but appreciate. Even the Obsidian Panther's coat showed off its glossy sheen as the Moon passed slowly overhead, giving the hunter time to reflect on how incredible a creature this predator was. Its body was nothing but lithe muscle, twisting every time the Panther made even the slightest movement. It was little wonder that it had been able to so easily track and chase him, even throughout the thick overgrowth of the jungle and injured so.

He shook away those thoughts quickly, blaming them on lack of sleep. Why, in this life threatening situation, would he admire the animal that would gladly rip his throat out given a moment's notice? Yet the Panther *still* hadn't done so, even though at this point Konta doubted he could so much as attempt to fight back if it decided to strike. It was a ponderous situation, to be sure. Konta spent the remainder of the night staring at his dozing foe, so lost in thought that he didn't even bother holding his knife out anymore.

At some point, Konta fell asleep because he was startled awake at a sudden gust of wind that hit his left. Without waiting to check what it was, he grabbed his knife with his injured hand and, ignoring the jolt of pain that shot through his arm, slashed out wildly.

His knife hit something hard, and an ear-splitting roar sounded from where he had randomly attacked. In a panic, Konta started to scuttle on his hands and knees, but only made it a couple paces before he put too much weight on his left hand and col- lapsed in pain, unable to fight through it anymore. To compound matters, he landed on his chest, tearing open the clotted wound and sending a fiery sensation through his body, nearly driving him unconscious. A steady stream of blood was already making its way across Konta's chest and running in rivulets across the blackened stone ground.

He turned weakly to see if maybe his panicked attack had driven off whatever had woken him up, but instead what met his sight was a lizard-like beast he had never seen before, not even in the tribe's picture accounts. Though roughly the same size as the Obsidian Panther and bearing scales with the same glassy black sheen, it stood on two legs at a height about equal to Konta. Its small arms ended in three clawed fingers, but Konta's attention was stolen by its mouth full of tiny needle-like teeth and the massive claws on its toes that put the Obsidian Panther's to shame.

It was only then that Konta realized that the aforementioned Panther was nowhere to be found. Undoubtedly, it had caught scent of this new predator and made haste to avoid the new creature. After all, the Panther had also been injured; why would it risk getting into a fight in such a condition?

As if arguing against Konta's thoughts, the Obsidian Panther suddenly lunged from the top of the ridge and began trying to maul the lizard beast. Dumbfounded, Konta could only watch as the two creatures rolled around, claws and teeth gnashing at each other as they tried to find purchase. The scales of the lizard seemed to be incredibly tough, with the Panther's claws unable to leave any more than minor gashes in the creature's skin. On the other hand, though the Panther's hide was also rather tough, it failed to provide the same level of protection, and multiple bites and slashes left deep bleeding wounds in the powerful feline.

Later in life, Konta would wonder constantly what inspired him to do what he did in that moment. As the Panther lay on the ground bleeding heavily, the lizard pounced in for the kill. It was so absorbed in the fight with the Obsidian Panther that it didn't notice Konta make an insane jump onto its back. As the creature screeched in surprise, Konta wildly began stabbing at the creature's eyes, a staple weakness of any beast with toughened skin. His hand wound sent jolts of pain through his whole body, but Konta was numb to it as his knife plunged downward over and over into the rapidly opening red gash that was once the reptilian predator's eye socket. Even after the monster collapsed, Konta continued to attack until the last of his desperate strength failed him and he rolled off the carcass gasping for breath.

His vision was beginning to blur, but he could still see as the Obsidian Panther slowly climb to its feet. Konta couldn't help but smile, knowing that there had never been any hope for him to escape from this situation alive in the first place. He closed his eyes, and sure enough, after a moment, he felt the pressure of jaws on his throat. They continued to tighten, but the crushing pain of fangs sinking in never came. Instead, he found himself pulled into a sitting position. Konta opened his eyes, an action that took far more effort than he wanted to expend at this point, and found the Panther staring at him, its eyes glinting as if examining him.

Konta tried to lay back down, exhausted as he was, but the Panther strode quickly behind him and started nudging him in the back. More confused than ever, Konta realized the Panther was *trying to get him to stand up.* This was something far beyond any experience he had as a hunter. From the earliest days he could remember, he was always taught to avoid all beasts no matter how great or small, that nothing other than a fellow tribesman could be trusted, and that everything was potentially deadly. Yet here was a creature that could finish him off without trying, but still he lived.

With nothing to lose at this point, Konta tried to force himself to stand. He managed to barely make it to his feet before he started to pitch forward in exhaustion, but the Panther caught him on its back. Too weary to think straight, Konta put his arm around the cat and held on almost by reflex. Surprisingly, the Panther seemed to have been waiting for this and began to walk as best it could with the injuries it had suffered. Konta normally would've assumed that it was dragging him back to its den, but with the way things were going he had no clue what to think anymore and instead let himself drift to sleep.

At one point he fell off the Obsidian Panther's back and woke with a jump, throwing his hands out to break the fall and almost crying in pain as most of his weight fell on his left hand. The Panther growled, a low and quiet call that almost sounded impatient as it nudged at Konta again and hissed. Konta did the only thing that made sense and crawled onto its back again, and once he had a good grip the Panther started forward once more. It was only now that

Konta realized the beast was dragging him through the jungle that it had chased him through. He found it hard to believe that it had only been yesterday that he had found the Nuevenceratops with his hunting brethren, and now he was being hauled bodily by a creature that had been trying to kill him until just recently.

Or had it been yesterday? Konta had no idea how long he had been asleep for. His stomach ached like he hadn't eaten in days. Could they really have been traveling that long? If that was the case, where in the world was this animal taking him?

His answer came only a short time later when he noticed some peculiar markings on a nearby rock. Hungry and tired as he was, it took him a few moments to recognize them as the obscure sketches his tribesmen made to indicate the village was nearby for hunters that got disoriented during hunts. His heart leapt into his throat, at first in fear. Perhaps the Panther had used his scent to find the village and all his people. If the Obsidian Panther's brethren attacked the tribe, even if his people managed to drive them off, the damage would be horrendous.

Yet Konta immediately dismissed the thought for some reason. He hadn't failed to notice that the Panther's wounds had not healed well during their trek, and still bled on occasion as it moved. He also had noticed that the other two Panthers that originally attacked with this particular one never returned from the jungle. Konta hoped vaguely that at least a cou-

227

ple of his fellow hunters had managed to stop the remaining Panthers and make it back safely.

His thoughts were cut short as the Obsidian Panther hit the ground hard. It was now that Konta realized the beast's breath was ragged and uneven, its emerald eyes rolling around glazed and unfocused. Realization washed over Konta in a great wave, and he shook his head in disbelief as he stared at the dying animal.

The Panther had taken him home.

It was such an insane idea, yet there was no other explanation. The Panther *had* used his scent most likely to find the village, but it was taking Konta back to his people. The why of the matter was impossible to figure out; was it grateful for him killing the lizard creature that almost killed it? *Could* it feel gratitude? Did it feel guilty for separating Konta from his people? How could a beast that ate the flesh of humans ever feel sympathy towards one?

Konta knew it was useless to figure out the why, but it was certain now that, whatever the motive, it had helped him. With that in mind, he didn't hesitate for a moment to pick up the great cat and throw it over his shoulder as he began to march towards the village. His body still hurt, his hand and chest gashes felt like they were reopening, and his stomach rumbled painfully, but the sleep he had caught up on during the trek had given enough energy to attempt this insane rescue. More than that, the desire to try and do anything he could to help his savior was all the drive he needed to push onward.

It was only a few minutes before the brush ahead of him began to shake. Two hunters stepped out with spears at the ready. At the sight of what Konta had slung across his back, the guards' eyes went wide and they hurried to his side. One of them took the Panther from him and hoisted it off towards the village. The other helped Konta steady himself and escorted him the same direction. Konta thought he saw a strange gleam of awe on the guard's face, but he was more worried about the condition of the Panther at this moment.

Konta had never seen a sight so welcoming as the sight of the tepees in the clearing they emerged into. Normally, the tribesmen would've been bustling about their duties at this time, but for some reason they had all gathered near the edge to greet Konta as he emerged. He stood, perplexed, as hunters clapped him on the shoulder and the tribeswomen half fawned over him and half fussed over his wounds.

As the tribeswomen dragged him away from the throng and towards the medical tent, Konta wearily wondered if they were trying to tend to the Panther at this moment too. It wasn't until he saw Murg approach and lay a gentle hand on his shoulder did Konta see the chief's feathered pelt, and all at once a wave of realization and nausea washed over him.

The next couple of days seemed to pass in an unreal rush for Konta. His wounds were cleaned and dressed, and at some point he had been led back to the fledgling's tent to rest, but all he could do was stare blankly at the ceiling until another uninitiated

hunter came in sometime after dark and pulled him
to the communal fire. Most of the village was milling
around the blaze, sharing food and some sort of fermented drink they kept saved for special occasions.
Konta was sat in the middle of the circling throng of
villagers, who immediately started forcing different
delicacies in front of him and not leaving him alone
until he at least tried each one.

After a short time, everyone suddenly stopped
moving, their heads turning expectantly to the back
of the group. The crowd parted to admit a wizened
old tribeswoman who was carefully carrying something dark and folded towards Konta. He knew perfectly well what it was long before it was set into his
arms.

A tight knot formed in his stomach as he looked at
the Obsidian Panther's face, which had been cured
into a hood for his new pelt. Its eyes were perfectly
preserved, a deep green that danced with the light
of the bonfire. Slowly he turned the whole pelt over
in his hands, noting the claws that were fastidiously
woven into the sleeve-like paws, giving him an extra
weapon if he so wished; the strong pads still attached
to the paws would keep their grip on any surface;
most notably, he realized how strong yet beautiful
the Panther's fur was, glassy and shimmering as the
communal fire danced.

He already knew what was expected of him next,
though he was loathe to do so. Slowly, he unfurled
the pelt in its entirety and draped it over his shoulders, making sure the hood rested snug on top of his

head. Though he couldn't see what it looked like for himself, he noticed some of the younger hunters he shared a tent with recoiling as if in fear, and he knew it must have struck a very intimidating pose on him.

Of course, this ceremony was the beginning of a whole new chapter of Konta's life. He was now a fully grown hunter in the eyes of the tribe and would be given all such amenities like his own tent and the consent of the chief to take a willing wife. More than that, a beast as rare and strong as the Obsidian Panther would give him considerably more status than the average newly pelted hunter; he would undoubtedly be considered one of the best among his fellow tribesmen.

And he knew that he hadn't earned any of it himself.

It was a futile effort to try and fight it, of course. There was no way he could communicate that he hadn't killed the creature but rather had accepted its help. Even if he could convey the message, it would be seen as a farce. The pelt was already on his shoulders, and little could be done to revoke it at this point. It simply never occurred to Konta that he could be so revolted from receiving what he had wanted so badly for so long.

As Murg led him to his new tent, Konta knew that the only way he could ever accept this gift of life and status he had received was to become the hunter the tribe now thought he was. No matter what happened in the future, however, he promised he would never forsake the pelt of the one who saved his life. That much, at least, he owed his strangest of friends.

Epilogue

Life is a precious thing that is often taken for granted. In the hustle and bustle of everyday living, most people just don't realize how their every action is, in fact, a fight for survival. But this wasn't always true.

Once, people cherished every moment that was given to them as they struggled to live to see just one more day, one more Sunrise. Sometimes, the cost was excruciating, and at times even unbearable, yet still they fought on in the face of overwhelming forces. In the end, they knew that no matter the pain or hardship, life always granted the chance at better days; death offered no such possibility.

As Konta walked among his people, the plant life rising all around them in warm welcome to the Spring of a new year, he realized how grateful he was to be alive. Here he was, against all the odds that had sought his destruction at the behest of numerous other creatures vying for survival, and he had managed to defy them and continue on regardless.

He had seen his fellow tribesmen fall to the same circumstances that had tried to claim his life. Each of these carved a deep wound in him that would one day scar over, yet never completely heal. Even so, now as he held his young pup Kontaren in his arms and strode side by side with his dear wife Kontala, he couldn't help but feel elation at the chance to be able to experience every single moment, to be allowed to see the fruits of his twenty plus Winters' experience desperately trying to survive.

As his tribe crested a hill, Konta paused for a moment at the top and let the wind brush across him blissfully. Kontala paused beside him and gave a small, puzzled smile. He grinned back and simply inhaled deeply in reply, taking in every little detail of the world that lay before him. It was a silly thing, a foolish thing, and no self-respecting hunter would've been caught dead doing something so strange.

But Konta wasn't like the other hunters, and he wouldn't want things to be any other way.

Tomorrow brings a new day and new challenges.

Dear reader,

We hope you enjoyed reading *Against All Instinct*. Please take a moment to leave a review, even if it's a short one. Your opinion is important to us.

Discover more books by Joshua Buller at https://www.nextchapter.pub/authors/joshua-buller

Want to know when one of our books is free or discounted? Join the newsletter at http://eepurl.com/bqqB3H

Best regards,
Joshua Buller and the Next Chapter Team

About the Author

Hey there! My name's Joshua, and I've been fascinated with storytelling practically since I was old enough to talk.

A bit about myself, I suppose. I'm in my early 30s, born and raised in Sacramento (that's the capital of California, in case you're confused). I'm the second of five children, and I. Love. Fantasy.

Growing up I was one of those kids who would blurt out the first thing that came to mind and got all the awkward stares. Even at the age of five, I could go on tangential rants for almost an hour that went nowhere.

In elementary school, I had my first brush with the dark side of fantasy: fan fiction. I spent several of my formative years writing stories based off of favorite TV shows and video games of mine.

This continued on through high school as a group of friends and I made a roleplaying forum where we tried to collaborate on writing a single narrative between almost a dozen people. It's about as easy as it sounds. Of course, it was moments like that that spurred me to eventually start trying my hand at writing original stories.

I've been working full time in the customer service industry since high school. It pays the bills, but doesn't give me a lot of time to write, so I usually have to really make it count when I can. When I'm not writing, I tend to be either reading or playing video games. Fantasy and sci-fi novels, Japanese manga, RPGs – if it has a fantastical element to it, I'm interested. Reading in particular has always been a huge passion of mine. There's nothing I enjoy more than a well told narrative and engaging characters.

On the other hand, I have a bit of a masochistic streak when it comes to movies and books as well. Oddly enough, I find immense satisfaction in reading a terrible book or watching a horrible movie. Well, part of that enjoyment probably comes from subjecting my friends to the same thing afterwards. Take it from me: if you show a friend Birdemic, and they're still friends with you after that, they're keepers.

My first book, *Against All Instinct*, started out as a writing exercise I was doing to try and create a narrative completely devoid of spoken dialogue. As I delved deeper and deeper into working on *AAI*, I found how enjoyable and rewarding it can be to put such restrictions on myself when creating a new piece.

I sincerely hope that people enjoy *Against All Instinct*, and know that this is just the beginning for me. There are dozens of other stories I'm dying to get out in the world, and if readers can find some enjoyment in what I create, then it's more than I could possibly hope for.

You might also like:

Assassins by David N. Pauly

To read the first chapter for free, please head to:
https://www.nextchapter.pub/books/assassins-the-
fourth-age-shadow-wars-epic-fantasy

Against All Instinct
ISBN: 978-4-86747-116-6 (Mass Market)

Published by
Next Chapter
1-60-20 Minami-Otsuka
170-0005 Toshima-Ku, Tokyo
+818035793528
17th May 2021